ACCLAIM FOR WENDI KAUFMAN'S
Helen on 86ᵗʰ Street and Other Stories

"Wendi Kaufman's widely anthologized and highly praised, perfect little bite-sized stories are captivating gems, full of remarkable and memorable characters. You will gobble them up and wish for more."
—**Ayelet Waldman**, *New York Times* best-selling author of *Love & Treasure* and *Red Hook Road*

"Wendi Kaufman's stories explore the tricky, glorious connections between men and women, mothers and daughters, sisters, fathers and daughters. In them, people often leave each other. They break each other's hearts. They realize how fleeting and fragile life is. And they triumph. Each story brings the reader a sense of hope in the end. A sense that, yeah, we can all keep going."
—**Ann Hood**, author of *The Obituary Writer* and *The Knitting Circle*

"Crafted with a light hand and deftly imagined, these stories bloom like tiny effervescent explosions in the mind. Delectable, insightful, a pure joy to read."
—**Janet Fitch**, *New York Times* best-selling author of *Paint It Black* and *White Oleander*

"With her charming, quirky characters and her mastery of the wry one-liner, Wendi Kaufman is proof of the human capacity to fall in love with a voice. This menagerie of women, from sly, sweet Vita of the title story to vulnerable Marie in 'Tryst and Doubt,' will stay with you long after the final page."
—**Susan Coll**, author of *The Stager* and *Beach Week*

"The characters in *Helen on 86th Street and Other Stories* are young, but they are wise and funny and observant and vulnerable, and they are drawn by Wendi Kaufman with such tenderness and care that they will live on with us, just as Kaufman herself will, long after we've read and reread this wonderful collection."

—**Joshua Henkin**, author of *The World Without You* and *Swimming Across the Hudson*

"Wendi Kaufman's wise, funny, beautifully structured stories get where they're going with a minimum of fuss, but the emotional currents run deep. She is a writer of rigor and tenderness who can find glints of grace in the most ordinary lives. I love this book."

—**Louis Bayard**, author of *Roosevelt's Beast* and *The Pale Blue Eye*

"Wendi Kaufman serves up the precious emotional truths of life as if they were a delicious meal, shared between the closest of friends. *Helen on 86th Street and Other Stories* is clear-eyed, big-hearted, and immensely entertaining."

—**Jami Attenberg**, *New York Times* best-selling author of *The Middlesteins* and *Instant Love*

"If a good novel is like a soup (go with me here), then the best short stories are bouillon cubes: complex flavors reduced to their essence. These are the kinds of stories Wendi Kaufman writes: She gives us tiny worlds, rich and self-contained, every element considered and necessary to the whole. She picks up her characters at the moment they need her most, and she stays with them until a half-beat before the reader is ready to let them go."

—**Carolyn Parkhurst**, author of *The Dogs of Babel* and *The Nobodies Album*

"While this debut collection, polished as beach glass, will break your heart many times over, Kaufman's fresh voice, unexpected humor, and deep understanding of the human condition will ultimately make you whole again."

—**Faye Moskowitz**, author of *And the Bridge Is Love* and *A Leak in the Heart*

"Wendi Kaufman's first story collection is an extraordinary debut. Her narrators, adults and children alike, try as hard as they can to make sense of the mysteries of love, marriage, and death in stories told with clear-eyed precision. It's a book both sad and funny, and always luminous and wise. I won't ever forget it."
—**Christopher Coake**, author of *We're in Trouble* and *You Came Back*

"These stories are by turns provocative, tender, sly, heartbreaking, and laugh-out-loud funny. Wendi Kaufman wields the twin knives of irony and insight with the expertise of a fencing master, and then salves the wounds with the deep compassion of a true healer."
—**Gary Krist**, author of *Empire of Sin* and *City of Scoundrels*

"Wendi Kaufman's depictions of childhood give me shivers, they are so piercingly authentic, but all of these stories are exquisite and each has, at its center, a hard, glowing core of hope. How I loved this book."
—**Marisa de los Santos**, *New York Times* best-selling author of *Love Walked In* and *Belong to Me*

"With a gift of brevity that will take your breath away, Wendi Kaufman's stories travel the universe of the heart in one sentence, then circle back again to reconsider that universe in the next sentence. From a young girl grieving for the father who abandoned her to the longing of that same girl to win the lead of Helen of Troy in a school play, there is so much beauty, wisdom, truth, and honesty in Kaufman's vision, her words go straight to the deepest source without interference. Simply stunning."
—**Jessica Keener**, author of *Night Swim* and *Women in Bed: Nine Stories*

"Wendi Kaufman's stories are courageous, funny, sad, disturbing, and, finally, deeply comforting. For some moments after I finished this book, I became, as one of her characters puts it, 'a child . . .who has seen, at the end of the day, the unsteady world put right.'"
—**David Huddle**, author of *Nothing Can Make Me Do This* and *The Story of a Million Years*

"In this debut collection, Wendi Kaufman delivers a world of characters as real as any I've encountered in as long as I can remember. Fatherless daughters, husbandless wives, lovers, ex-lovers—a world teeming with poignancy and heartbreak and that rarest of all qualities, humor. The voices of Kaufman's characters call out from the page. I didn't just read them; I heard them. What a generous, tender, wildly perceptive writer we have here. Wendi Kaufman's sharp eye takes in everything—makes us shudder and smile. She's got an ear as perfectly on-key as a tuning fork. I love this writer."

—**Joyce Maynard**, *New York Times* best-selling author of *After Her* and *Labor Day*

"The characters who live inside Wendi Kaufman's stories are funny, frightened, damaged, and redeemed, their world a cascade of familial and romantic tumult rendered so elegantly, so viciously, that it's almost impossible to imagine they'll ever get out alive. But they do. They do! *Helen on 86th Street and Other Stories* is a collection that crosses the intersection of life's great expectations and great failures and never pulls back, never lets go, and the result is nothing short of revelatory."

—**Tod Goldberg**, author of *Gangsterland* and *Living Dead Girl*

"Wendi Kaufman's stories, whether short sketches or those that go for longer stretches, glitter with detail, not just in her prose but in the lives captured by that prose. In chronicling the travails of families—traditional families, unconventional ones, children at odds with parents, parents at odds with themselves—Kaufman can break your heart, but she can also rebuild it."

—**Ben Greenman**, author of *The Slippage* and *What He's Poised to Do*

"Wendi Kaufman is a writer who clearly knows a great deal about both wonder and despair. Like the skillfully drawn character of Vita in her much-loved title story 'Helen on 86th Street,' Ms. Kaufman's prose evokes amazement at the mysteries of this world and its conventions. My favorite character in that story, however, is Vita's mother, whose sadness is as palpable as her strength. She's the kind of character a reader dreams of meeting in the real world. That, of course, is impossible, which makes me even more grateful for the story. It's a gift, as is this long-awaited collection."

—**Edward Falco**, author of *Toughs* and *Burning Man: Stories*

"'Helen on 86th Street' is a beautiful story. Even the humor, and it is bursting with humor, is beautiful. There is an amiable intensity and comic intelligence to Wendi Kaufman's writing that lets us understand and honor the reality of imagination. The work is tart and understated, powerful in its sympathy and warmth, and did I mention that it's funny as hell? It is funny as hell."

—**Cathleen Schine**, author of *The Three Weissmanns of Westport* and *The New Yorkers*

"Wendi Kaufman recognizes that our child and adult selves coexist, often uncomfortably, and she zeroes in on those telling moments when the distinction blurs. In one story, a girl is ushered prematurely into the world of adult dysfunction. In another, a woman navigates the obstacle course of adultery. The people in this collection cross Rubicons both recognized and unrecognized: Patterns repeat, things come full circle, past and present coexist. Many of these gently nuanced pieces explore everyday life with an overlay of allegory and mythology and demonstrate how art both emerges from and is intertwined with it. Stories alternately funny and poignant explore the chromatics of abandonment; the resonance of divorce; the sustenance of family—what Kaufman calls 'love and loss entwined, a knotted tangle of grief and desire.'"

—**Nicole Arthur**, Editor, *The Washington Post*

"Exquisitely written, and deeply moving, Kaufman's debut reads like the work of a seasoned master in a brilliant collection of stories about loss, love, and longing, all with a quirky sensibility that's funny, poignant, and heart-wrenchingly redemptive, too."

—**Caroline Leavitt**, *New York Times* best-selling author of *Is This Tomorrow* and *Pictures of You*

"*Helen on 86th Street and Other Stories* is a pleasure to read, rewarding to ponder, just the right mix of wisdom and wisecracking—one of those rare literary gems that will appeal to a wide range of smart readers, from the *Fault in Our Stars* set to the savviest wine bar book club and countless airplanes and beaches in between."

—**Joni Rodgers**, *New York Times* best-selling author of *Sugarland* and *The Hurricane Lover*

"If you are a woman of a certain age—that is, you remember sitting in the front seat of the family car while your parents smoked beside you—this collection will make you weep. A delightful trip down emotional and cultural memory lanes. This one stays on the bedside table."

—**Karen Bergreen**, author of *Perfect Is Overrated* and *Following Polly*

"In these wry and tender stories, Wendi Kaufman beautifully describes the ties that bind lovers, friends, and, most of all, family— ties so tight that sometimes they almost break us, too. Like the writing of one of her protagonists, her work 'tastes only like truth to the mouth.'"

—**Natalie Danford**, author of *Inheritance*

"A gorgeous collection from a writer of sure grace and rare voice. Headlined by the extraordinary 'Helen on 86th Street,' Kaufman's stories are subtle and elegant. She navigates the tricky landscape of the human heart, exploring the fine, frail connections that exist in families—the ways they break and the ways they save us. Her voice shines through each tale, infused with a wry, smart wit that makes this whole collection a pure reading pleasure."

—**Joshilyn Jackson**, *New York Times* best-selling author of *Someone Else's Love Story* and *Between, Georgia*

Author photograph by Elizabeth Osborne

WENDI KAUFMAN's fiction has appeared in *The New Yorker, Fiction, New York Stories, Other Voices,* and *Ascent.* Her stories have been anthologized in *Scribner's Best of the Fiction Workshops, Elements of Literature,* and *Faultlines: Stories of Divorce.* Recipient of a literary fellowship from the Virginia Commission for the Arts, winner of a Mary Roberts Rinehart award for short fiction, and named a Breadloaf Writers' Conference David Sokolov Scholar in Fiction, she is also a frequent contributor to *The Washington Post* and *The Washingtonian* and holds an MFA in Creative Writing from George Mason University. *Helen on 86ᵗʰ Street and Other Stories* is her first story collection.

Home is where our story begins. To David, Alexander, and Eli.
Always and forever.

The power to change one's life comes from a paragraph, a lone remark. The lines that penetrate us are slender, like the flukes that live in river water and enter the bodies of swimmers . . . How can we imagine what our lives should be without the illumination of the lives of others?

James Salter, *Light Years*

Helen on 86th Street and Other Stories

Wendi Kaufman

stillhouse
press

Stillhouse Press

Fairfax, Virginia
George Mason University

FIRST EDITION

**stillhouse
press**

"Helen on 86th Street" first appeared in *Scribner's Best of the Fiction Workshops 1998*, guest edited by Carol Shields. It was later republished in different form in *The New Yorker*; the textbook *Elements of Literature*; and the anthology *Fault Lines: Stories of Divorce*; and was adapted into a musical, available at www.playscripts.com. "Life Above Sea Level" first appeared in *Other Voices*. "Tryst and Doubt" originally appeared as "Adulterer's Delight" in *Enhanced Gravity: More Fiction by Washington Area Women*. "True Confessions of a Bread Baker" appeared in *Literal Latte*. "Pressure System" appeared in *New York Stories*. "Talk" appeared in *Parting Gifts*. "Significant Other" appeared in *Fiction* magazine. "Intimate Landscape" appeared in *Literary Mama*. "What Remains" appeared in *Ascent*.

Stillhouse Press
4400 University Drive, 3E4
Fairfax, VA 22030
www.stillhousepress.org
editor@stillhousepress.org

Stillhouse Press is a nonprofit literary organization established in collaboration with George Mason University's Creative Writing MFA program and Northern Virginia's Fall for the Book literary festival.

**Library of Congress Control Number: 2014944826
ISBN-10: 0-9905169-0-3
ISBN-13: 978-0-9905169-0-3**

*Art direction and cover design by Paul Gormont: Apertures, Inc.
Interior layout by Kady Dennell*

Printed in the United States of America

Contents

INTRODUCTION
Mary Kay Zuravleff

Finishing a Wendi Kaufman story, one is tempted to rise from one's seat, applauding and calling out in praise: *That voice!* Singularly shrewd and insightful, Wendi hits many of the same notes in these fourteen stories, alternating her pitch just enough to give voice to dozens of women at different ages. Distinct from the mostly first-person narrators of these stories, the author is vividly present. Not intrusive, not self-conscious. Present, in the most genuine and generous sense of the word. Who can pay such astonishing attention? In a collection of stories, Wendi's talent is important because her stories reveal the solidarity as well as the singularity of women. Two sisters with little in common; the other woman who learns about the other other woman; daughters and mothers left behind—Wendi sings full-throatedly of them all. And after each story, hands red from clapping, readers will want to scramble right back into their seats to hear the next and then the next.

Let's take it from the opening number, where Vita, our narrator, is indignant because the most beautiful, flirty girl in the sixth grade has been cast as Helen of Troy. Just above Vita's outrage is a worldly, sardonic descant—the head guy picking beauty over brains is an old story. In fact, Vita's father is away "on his own odyssey" (men in this collection have weak or fickle hearts), and when Vita's mother chimes in halfway between Vita's outrage and the author's resignation, we get a full chord. "You want to know about Helen?" Vita's mother asks. "Well, her father was a swan and her mother was too young to have children. You don't want to be Helen. Be lucky you're a warrior. You're too smart to be ruled by your heart."

Like an elbow in the ribs is the narrator, reminding us that intelligent women overruled by their hearts is a mainstay of literature. Whether of life is for you to decide—Wendi regularly undermines such conceits as her characters pine to act out the oldest stories people tell. Of course, what is clear upon reflection is still taking shape while reading. That's how metaphor works. Adding the scrim of mythology to the stage complicates the reading and clarifies the reflection.

Bernard Malamud, in a *Paris Review* interview, explained this miracle in his own work. "I love metaphor. It provides two loaves where there seems to be one. Sometimes it throws in a load of fish. The mythological analogy is a system of metaphor. It enriches the vision without resorting to montage . . . You relate to the past and predict the future."

"Helen on 86th Street," the title story in this collection, has enjoyed a wide following since it appeared, in slightly different forms, both in *The New Yorker* in 1997 and in *Scribner's Best of the Fiction Workshops 1998*. Ninth graders read it in their literature textbooks, and, in 2011, lyricist Nicole Kempskie and composer Robby Stamper adapted it into a musical. So a story about the ages becomes one for the ages.

May there be more musicals and movies as well made from Wendi's work. Start with "Visitation Rights," please, in which Missy cracks wise about a promised visit from her dead grandmother. "'I wouldn't joke if I were you,' my mother says. 'And if that's the case, I would clean up a little bit before she gets here.' My mother looks around my tiny room. 'She was always such a pain in the ass about clutter.'" That story is as much Lorrie Moore as it is Bernard Malamud. Were I tracing Kaufman's literary genealogy, I might suggest she was Malamud and Moore's literary love child, though analogies to literary sisters, mothers, and grandmothers might be more appropriate considering her subject matter.

Kaufman can make a Moore-ish aphorism of agony, such as the girl in "Still Life" downplaying her mother's depression: "She's calling her time on the couch a victory for furniture." It is awkwardness, however, that Moore cites as her greatest source of humor. Here's the jilted mistress Wendi dreamed up in "Tryst and Doubt": "The definition of karma is helping your lover come up with a good alibi for his wife about his late-night whereabouts and then having that same excuse used on you later." Awkward, sad, funny. As Moore said in her *Paris Review* interview, "Storymaking aside, in real life people are always funny. Or, people are always funny eventually. It would be dishonest to pretend not to notice."

We want the people in our lives to make good choices. Not so in our fiction. Bad behavior makes for poignant, hilarious, and even instructive antics. And so arrives this book by a writer famous for her generosity, a live wire and best friend to many, a woman who has been joyously hitched for thirty-plus years to a man she married at eighteen. Fortunately, Wendi Kaufman imagines herself into other women's lives and takes us along, and our rousing ovation will serve as a testament to a life of profound creativity and talent, lived with a rare love of family, friends, and literature.

Applause is also in order for Stillhouse Press. Founded by Dallas Hudgens of Relegation Books, the press is run by George Mason University MFA students, who learn publishing as well as promotion, an essential skill for today's writers. It is right and meet and fitting that Wendi's stories teach students about word of mouth, because she has done the same for so many. Wendi used her raucous, big-hearted blog, "The Happy Booker," as a cyber-megaphone, championing writers she enjoys and admires. Devoted, in her words, to "people speaking books as a second language," she was anointed by Fairfax County, Virginia, to discuss All Fairfax Reads with hundreds of library-goers, which led to the Literature & Medicine program to boost doctors' empathy and compassion and the juvenile offender program, Changing Lives through Literature. Wendi regularly assigned "her girls" important scenes in novels to rewrite, "an exercise that allows them to reinvent themselves"; during the last session, they read in front of their families as well as a judge and the court official who "sentenced" them to the program.

Wendi has also known when and how to close ranks and make a safe community for setting deadlines, offering criticism, and reading innumerable drafts. Upon graduation from GMU in 1997, she and four MFA classmates formed the Rotisserie Writers Group (named for the chicken). Their motto is "We meet as a group or we don't meet," and they have managed to gather ten times a year—for seventeen years. This group has seen one another through marriages, divorces, kids from birth through graduation and beyond, and some half-dozen books. They have, in fact, seen Wendi Kaufman through her entire writing life, up to and including the collection you are holding in your hands.

I

HELEN ON 86TH STREET

I hate Helen. That's all I can say. I hate her. Helen McGuire
is playing Helen, so Mr. Dodd says, because, out of the entire
sixth grade, she most embodies Helen of Troy. Great. Helen
McGuire has no idea who Helen of Troy even was! When she
found out, well, you should have seen her—flirting with all the
boys, really acting the part. And me? Well, I know who Helen
was. I am pissed.

My mother doesn't understand. Not that I expected she
would. When I tell her the news, all she says is, "Ah, the face
that launched a thousand ships." She doesn't even look up
from her book. Later, at dinner, she apologizes for quoting
Marlowe. Marlowe is our cat.

At bedtime I tell my mother, "You should have seen the way
Helen acted at school. It was disgusting, flirting with the boys."

Mom tucks the sheets up close around my chin, so only my
head is showing, my body covered mummy style. "Vita," she
says, "it sounds like she's perfect for the part."

So, I can't play Helen. But, to make it worse, Mr. Dodd said
I have to be in the horse. I can't believe it. The horse! I wanted
to be one of the Trojan women—Andromache, Cassandra, or
even Hecuba. I know all their names. I told Mr. Dodd this, and

then I showed him I could act. I got really sad and cried out about the thought of the body of my husband, Hector, being dragged around the walls of my city. I wailed and beat my fist against my chest. "A regular Sarah Heartburn," was all he said.

"Well, at least you get to be on the winning team," my mother says when I tell her about the horse. This doesn't make me feel any better. "It's better than being Helen. It's better than being blamed for the war," she tells me.

Mom is helping me make a shield for my costume. She says every soldier had a shield that was big enough to carry his body off the field. I tell her I'm not going to be a body on the field, that I am going to survive, return home.

"Bring the shield, just in case," she says. "It never hurts to have a little help."

Mom and I live on West Eighty-sixth Street. We have lived in the same building, in the same apartment, my entire life. My father has been gone for almost three years. The truth is that he got struck with the wanderlust—emphasis on "lust," my mother says—and we haven't heard from him since.

"Your father's on his own odyssey," my mother says. And now it's just me and Mom and Marlowe and the Keatses, John and John, our parakeets, or "pair of Keats" as Mom says. When I was younger, when Dad first left and I still believed he was coming back, it made me happy that we still lived in the same building. I was happy because he would always know where to find us. Now that I am older, I know the city is not that big. It is easy to be found and easy to stay lost.

And I also know not to ask about him. Sometimes Mom hears things through old friends—that he has travelled across the ocean, that he is living on an island in a commune with some people she calls "the lotus eaters," that he misses us.

Once I heard Mr. Farfel, the man who's hanging around Mom now, ask why she stayed in this apartment after my father left. "The rent's stabilized," she told him, "even if the relationship wasn't."

At school, Helen McGuire is acting weird because I'm going to be in the horse with Tommy Aldridge. She wants to know what it's like: "Is it really cramped in there? Do you have to sit real close together?"

I tell her it's dark, and we must hold each other around the waist and walk to make the horse move forward. Her eyes grow wide at this description. "Lucky you," she says.

Lucky me? She gets to stand in the center of the stage alone, her white sheet barely reaching the middle of her thighs, and say lines like "This destruction is all my fault," and "Paris, I do love you." She gets to cry. Why would she think I'm lucky? The other day at rehearsal, she was standing onstage waiting for her cue, and I heard Mrs. Reardon, the stage manager, whisper, "That Helen is as beautiful as a statue."

At home Old Farfel is visiting again. He has a chair in Mom's department. The way she describes it, a chair is a very good thing. Mom translates old books written in Greek and Latin. She is working on the longest graduate degree in the history of Columbia University. "I'll be dead before I finish," she always says.

Old Farfel has been coming around a lot lately, taking Mom and me to dinner at Italian places downtown and telling Mom jokes with strange punchlines—*vidi, vici, veni*; they laugh strangely when I tell them it's in the wrong order. I don't like to be around when he's over.

"I'm going to Agamemnon's apartment to rehearse," I tell Mom.

Old Farfel makes a small laugh, one that gets caught in the back of the throat and never really makes it out whole. I want to tell him to relax, to let it out. He smells like those dark cough drops, the kind that make your eyes tear and your head feel like it's expanding. I don't know how she can stand him.

"Well, the play's the *thing*," Old Farfel says. "We're all just players strutting and fretting our hour on the stage." Mom smiles at this, and it makes me wish Old Farfel would strut his hours at his apartment and not at our place. I hate the way he's beginning to come around all the time.

When I get back from rehearsal, Mom is spinning Argus. It's what she does when she gets into one of her moods. Argus, our dog, died last summer when I was away at camp. My mother can't stand to part with anything, so she keeps Argus, at least his ashes, in a blue-and-white vase that sits on our mantel.

Once I looked into the vase. I'd expected to see gray stuff, like the ash at the end of a cigarette. Instead, there was black sand and big chunks of pink like shells, just like at the beach.

My mother has the vase down from the mantel and is twirling it in her hands. I watch the white figures on it turn, following each other, running in a race that never ends.

"Life is a cycle," my mother says. The spinning makes me dizzy. I don't want to talk about life. I want to talk about Helen.

"Helen, again with Helen. Always Helen," my mother says. "You want to know about Helen?"

I nod my head.

"Well, her father was a swan and her mother was too young to have children. You don't want to be Helen. Be lucky you're a warrior. You're too smart to be ruled by your heart."

"And what about beauty? Wasn't she the most beautiful woman in the world?" I ask.

Mom looks at the Greek vase. "Beauty is truth, truth beauty—that is all ye need to know."

She is not always helpful.

"Manhattan is a rocky island," Mom says at dinner. "There is no proper beach, no shore." My mother grew up in the South, near the ocean, and there are times when she still misses the beach. Jones, Brighton, or even Coney Island beaches don't come close for her. I know when she starts talking about the water that she's getting restless. I hope this means that Old Farfel won't be hanging around too long.

Every night I write a letter to my father. I don't send them—I don't know where to send them—but, still, I write them. I keep the letters at the back of my closet in old shoeboxes. I am on my third box. It's getting so full that I have to keep the lid tied down with rubber bands.

I want to write, "Mom is talking about the water again. I think this means she is thinking of you. We are both thinking of you, though we don't mention your name. Are you thinking of us? Do you ever sit on the shore at night and wonder what we're doing, what we're thinking? Do you miss us as much as we miss you?"

But instead I write, "I am in a play about the Trojan War. I get to wear a short white tunic, and I ambush people from inside a big fake horse. Even though we win the war, it will be many, many years before I return home. Until I see my family again. In this way, we are the same. I will have many adventures. I will meet giants and witches and see strange lands. Is that what you are doing? I wish you could come to the play."

Old Farfel is going to a convention in Atlanta. He wants Mom to go with him. From my bed, I can hear them talking about it in the living room. It would be good for her, he says. I know that Mom doesn't like to travel. She can't even go to school and back without worrying about the apartment—if she turned the gas off, if she fed the cat, if she left me enough money. She tells him that she'll think about it.

"You have to move on, Victoria," he tells her. "Let yourself go to new places."

"I'm still exploring the old places," she says.

He lets the conversation drop.

Mom said once that she travelled inside herself when Dad left. I didn't really understand, but it was one of the few times I saw her upset. She was sitting in her chair, at her desk, looking tired. "Mom, are you in there?" I waved my hand by her face.

"I'm not," she said. "I'm on new ground. It's a very different place."

"Are you thinking about Dad?"

"I was thinking how we all travel differently, Vita. Some of us don't even have to leave the house."

"Dad left the house."

"Sometimes it's easier to look outside than in," she said.

That night I dream about a swan. A swan that flies in circles over the ocean. This is not the dark water that snakes along the West Side Highway and slaps against the banks of New Jersey, but the real ocean. Open water. Salty, like tears.

At play practice, I watch the other girls dress up as goddesses and Trojan women. They wear gold scarves wound tight around their necks and foreheads. They all wear flowers in their hair and flat pink ballet slippers. I wear a white sheet taken from my bed. It is tied around the middle with plain white rope. I also wear white sneakers. I don't get to wear a gold scarf or flowers. Mr. Dodd wrote this play himself and is very picky about details. Tommy Aldridge, my partner in the horse, was sent home because his sheet had Ninja Turtles on it. "They did not have Ninja Turtles in ancient Greece," Mr. Dodd said.

Mr. Dodd helps Helen McGuire with her role. "You must understand," he tells her, "Helen is the star of the show. Men have travelled great distances just to fight for her. At the end, when you come onstage and look at all the damage you've caused, we must believe you're really upset by the thought that this is all your fault."

Helen nods and looks at him blankly.

"Well, at least try to think of something really sad."

Old Farfel is taking Mom out to dinner again. It's the third time this week. Mom says it is a very important dinner, and I am not invited. Not that I would want to go, but I wasn't even asked. Mom brought in takeout, some soup and a cheese sandwich, from the coffee shop on the corner.

I eat my soup, alone in the kitchen, from a blue-and-white paper cup. I remember once at a coffee shop Mom held the same type of cup out in front of me.

"See this building, Vita?" she said. She pointed to some columns that were drawn on the front of her cup. It wasn't really a building—more like a cartoon drawing. "It's the Parthenon," she said. "It's where the Greeks made sacrifices to Athena."

"How did they make sacrifices?" I asked.

"They burned offerings on an altar. They believed this would bring them what they wanted. Good things. Luck."

I finish my soup and look at the tiny building on the cup. In between the columns are the words "Our Pleasure to Serve You." I run my fingers across the flat lines of the Parthenon and trace the roof. I can almost imagine a tiny altar and the ceremonies that were performed there.

It is then that I get an idea. I find a pair of scissors on Mom's desk and cut through the thick white lip of the cup toward the lines of the little temple. I cut around the words "Our Pleasure to Serve You." Then I take the temple and the words and glue them to the back of my notebook. The blue-

and-white lines show clearly against the cardboard backing. I get Argus's big metal water bowl from the kitchen and find some matches from a restaurant Old Farfel took us to for dinner.

In my room I put on my white sheet costume and get all my letters to Dad out from the back of the closet. I know that I must say something, to make this more like a ceremony. I think of any Greek words I know: *spanakopita, moussaka, gyro.* They're only food words, but it doesn't matter. I decide to say them anyway. I say them over and over out loud until they blur into a litany, my own incantation: "*Spanakopitamoussakaandgyro, spanakopitamoussakaandgyro, spanakopitamoussakaandgyro.*"

As I say this, I burn handfuls of letters in the bowl. I think about what I want: to be Helen, to have my father come back. Everything I have ever heard says that wishes are granted in threes, so I throw in the hope of Old Farfel's leaving.

I watch as the words burn. Three years of letters go up in smoke and flame. I see blue-lined paper turn to black ashes; I see pages and pages, months and years, burn, crumble, and then disappear. The front of my white sheet has turned black from soot, and my eyes water and burn.

When I am done, I take the full bowl of ashes and hide it in the vase on the mantel, joining it with Argus. My black hands smudge the white figures on the vase, until their tunics become as sooty as my own. I change my clothes and open all the windows, but still Mom asks, when she comes home, about the burning smell. I tell her I was cooking.

She looks surprised. Neither of us cooks much. "No more burnt offerings when I'm not home," she says. She looks upset and distracted, and Old Farfel doesn't give that stifled laugh of his.

It's all my fault. Helen McGuire has chicken pox. Bad. She has been out of school for almost two weeks. I know my burning ceremony did this. "The show must go on," Mr. Dodd said when Achilles threw up the tater tots or when Priam's beard got caught in Athena's hair, but this is different. This is Helen. And it's my fault.

I know all her lines. Know them backward and forward. I have stood in our living room, towel tied around my body, and acted out the entire play, saying every line for my mother. When Mr. Dodd makes the announcement about Helen at dress rehearsal, I stand up, white bedsheet slipping from my shoulders, and say in a loud clear voice, "The gods must have envied me my beauty, for now my name is a curse. I have become hated Helen, the scourge of Troy."

Mr. Dodd shakes his head and looks very sad. "We'll see, Vita. She might still get better," he says.

Helen McGuire recovers, but she doesn't want to do the part because of all the pockmarks that are left. Besides, she wants to be inside the horse with Tommy Aldridge. Mr. Dodd insists that she still be Helen until her parents write that they don't want her to be pressured, they don't want to *do any further damage*, whatever that means. After that, the part is mine.

Tonight is the opening, and I am so excited. Mom is coming without Old Farfel. "He wasn't what I wanted," she said. I don't think she'll be seeing him anymore.

"What is beautiful?" I ask Mom before the play begins.

"Why are you so worried all the time about beauty? Don't you know how beautiful you are to me?"

"Would Daddy think I was beautiful?"

"Oh, Vita, he *always* thought you were beautiful."

"Would he think I was like Helen?"

She looks me up and down, from the gold lanyard snaked through my thick hair to my too-tight pink ballet slippers.

"He would think you're more beautiful than Helen. I'm almost sorry he won't be here to see it."

"*Almost* sorry?"

"Almost. At moments like this—you look so good those ancient gods are going to come alive again with envy."

"What do you mean, come alive again? What are you saying about the gods?"

"Vita, Greek polytheism is an extinct belief," she says, and laughs. And then she stops and looks at me strangely. "When people stopped believing in the gods, they no longer had power. They don't exist anymore. You must have known that."

Didn't I get the part of Helen? Didn't Old Farfel leave? I made all these things happen with my offering. I know I did. I don't believe these gods disappeared. At least not Athena.

"I don't believe you."

She looks at me, confused.

"You can't know for sure about the gods. And who knows? Maybe Daddy will even be here to see it."

"Sure," she says. "And maybe this time the Trojans will win the war."

I stand offstage with Mr. Dodd and wait for my final cue. The dry-ice machine has been turned on full blast and an incredible amount of fake smoke is making its way toward the painted backdrop of Troy. Hector's papier-mâché head has accidentally slipped from Achilles's hand and is now making a hollow sound as it rolls across the stage.

I peek around the thick red curtain, trying to see into the audience. The auditorium is packed, filled with parents and camcorders. I spot my mom sitting in the front row, alone. I try to scan the back wall, looking for a sign of him, a familiar shadow. Nothing.

Soon I will walk out on the ramparts, put my hand to my forehead, and give my last speech. "Are you sure you're ready?" Mr. Dodd asks. I think he's more nervous than I am. "Remember," he tells me, "this is Helen's big moment. Think loss." I nod, thinking nothing.

"Break a leg," he says, giving me a little push toward the stage. "And try not to trip over the head."

The lights are much brighter than I expected, making me squint. I walk through the smoky fog toward center stage.

"It is I, the hated Helen, scourge of Troy."

With the light on me, the audience is in shadow, like a big pit, dark and endless. I bow before the altar, feeling my tunic rise. "Hear my supplication," I say, pulling down a bit on the back of my tunic.

"Do not envy me such beauty—it has wrought only pain and despair."

I can hear Mr. Dodd, offstage, loudly whispering each line along with me.

"For this destruction, I know I will be blamed."

"Blamed," Mr. Dodd whispers. His timing is a beat behind mine.

I begin to recite Helen's wrongs—beauty, pride, the abdication of Sparta—careful to enunciate clearly. "Troy, I have come to ask you to forgive me."

I'm supposed to hit my fist against my chest, draw a hand across my forehead, and cry loudly. Mr. Dodd has shown me this gesture, practiced it with me in rehearsal a dozen times— the last line, my big finish. The audience is very quiet. In the stillness there is a hole, an empty pocket, an absence. Instead of kneeling, I stand up, straighten my tunic, look toward the audience, and speak the line softly: "And to say good-bye."

There is a prickly feeling up the back of my neck. And then applause. The noise surrounds me, filling me. I look into the darkened house and, for a second, I can hear the beating of a swan's wings, and, then, nothing at all.

LIFE ABOVE SEA LEVEL

patchogue 1968

"Sink or swim," my mother's brother says as he drops me from the side of a boat in the Great South Bay. Bobbing up, head above water, I can see the shore, see where my father sits in a folding chair, *Times* spread across his lap, head tipped back, eyes closed. Water fills my nose and lungs, and I am scooped out by a strong-armed uncle. Funny, they said, it worked so well with all the other kids.

Every summer my mother's family piles into this house bought by a grandfather, great uncles, and an aunt. My mother's family: police detectives, payroll clerks, and Brooklyn Navy Yard workers. Irish. This is a place where men come to catch blues, weekend fishermen after a perfect run. Where women wash clothes in ice-cold water, then hang them on long lines cast toward the Bay. Line-dried clothes, stiff and hard, that stink of bay water and don't bend easily against skin.

I am spending the weekend with my parents at this house, a four-room summer bungalow with an old outhouse and a hand-cranked pump in the kitchen with water so cold it makes my teeth ache. Nights when the weather turns cool the house is kept warm with a kerosene heater. The smell burns my nose and clings to my clothes.

My parents spend much of this visit away from the bungalow taking long car rides. They drive with the windows rolled down, me sitting between them in the front seat, my thighs sticking to the red vinyl cushion, my hands reaching out for the large silver radio knobs.

"Why did we come here?" my mother asks after my near-drowning. She flicks a cigarette ash out the window. She repeats the question, even though my father and I don't answer.

We drive back roads that take us far from my mother's family, far from the bottles of alcohol stored in tall fisherman boots by the back door and in the mop bucket under the bathroom sink. Far from the endless games of gin rummy where men sit on the open-air porch playing cards and making jokes about my father chasing ambulances and robbing cradles.

My mother likes to stop at roadside stands and small shacks with large red signs that read FRESH! Places where the strong smell of clams and mussels lingers in the air. Men in undershirts drag boxes of clams off the backs of trucks, shuck them roadside, and drop them in large kettles of boiling water.

My mother holds the clamshell to her mouth, scoops the fleshy part out with her teeth. "It's best when you can still taste the sand," she says. "When you can feel the grit against your teeth."

My father doesn't eat. Raised kosher, he has no taste for the hard-shelled fish that spends its life hiding away from harm.

fire island 1973

Past Patchogue, past my mother's family that we do not visit, to catch the ferry. *Fair Harbor.* When the boat lands, luggage, food, and my brothers, two plump-legged babies, are loaded into sturdy red wagons and pulled over the wooden slat walkway to our house. There are no cars on the island. Here is a new sound for us, the loud sound of quiet not heard in the city.

My parents' friends visit on weekends. They say *marvelous* or *delightful* when they see the house. But it's when they step onto the deck that they point wildly at the ocean, ice clinking against the sides of their glasses, and always say the same thing: *What a view!*

Every evening the sunset is celebrated. An event. My father mixes drinks, pours them from a thick-lipped silver shaker, for the lined-up visitors. My mother doesn't take ice. Why water down a good thing? she says. Nice and neat, just like you, he always says when he hands her a glass. These are the lines they know by heart.

My mother takes her nightly place on the deck, my small brothers resting against each hip, and leans on the rail for support. It is the first time each day that we turn our back to the ocean, face west and wait for dark.

"Our family is just drawn to the water," my father says as the light fades. "It's our legacy."

coney island 1979

Shaina maideleh, my aunt calls me in front of her friends. Pretty girl. Marriageable girl. I am visiting my aunt's cabana at Brighton Beach. It is past the season, and she is dressed warmly to sit outside and play mah-jongg. Her friends, women she has known for forty years, stop playing for a moment to look me up and down. Their thick-veined hands never far from the smooth tiles.

"Why do you want to go over there for?" My aunt argues with my father. "What's to see?" She is trying to talk him out of a short trip to Coney Island before we return to the city.

"It's not how you remember it," she warns him. "Things are different now."

But this is time for good-byes. My father is packing up his law practice, retiring, moving away from the city with us. He doesn't want to hear what my aunt has to tell him, his mind on the Coney Island of memory: the original Nathan's, the aquarium, the amusement park. Our subway ride is filled with stories that begin, "Did I ever tell you about the time…" The train leaves its subterranean tracks and heads above ground. We are elevated, getting closer to the water.

He wants to take me to where he grew up, where he spent hot afternoons walking the crowded beaches, escaping his strict orthodox home. Here's where Saul used to live and the Greenfarbs, he'll tell me, my head reeling with the stories of stickball players and egg creams. Instead we're greeted by boarded-up storefronts, a beach community battening down the hatches before the storm. Graffiti and broken bottles overtake the landscape. It's fall at the beach, after the season. Russian women in black push past us, darting into neighborhood stores with Cyrillic signs.

The dark comes early. My father and I catch the train home. He doesn't speak on our ride back, no more stories, just the smell of salt water and the memory of the littered shoreline.

seaside heights 1983

New Jersey. Down the shore. Home to girls with the highest hair I have ever seen, moussed, sticking straight up from their foreheads. This is the boardwalk: bright lights, skee-ball, and the smell of fried fish. Friends and friends of friends piled into a car and crossing state lines looking for adventure. At night, sunburned skin stinging, I am alone on the beach with a boy. He kisses me, slips his hands under my shirt and tells me he loves me. My heart swells. Somewhere in the background a Bruce Springsteen song is playing.

At home bright lights of an ambulance carry my father away. The first of many heart attacks. I return to an empty house and a note written by my mother with directions to the hospital. I can picture her frantically searching for something to write with, saying, as she walks in circles, how can we live in a house without pens, how can we live like this? Her note is weighed down with a heavy crystal tumbler, her empty drink glass.

sag harbor 1986

As soon as the weather turns warm the tap water in my one-room apartment on West Fourth turns brown—water main breakage, the harbinger of a long New York City summer. I am offered a trade: my city apartment for a friend's guest cottage on Long Island.

The island air is cooler. I sleep with the windows open on an old metal bed that pulls down from the wall—only the weight of my body pressed against the wall will keep the bed from becoming airborne, its legs threatening to rear up like a prop in an old vaudeville skit. I work waitress jobs and live a life with no phone. Letters begin to carry weight and I start to check my mailbox every day.

It is my mother's brief notes, ones written on spiral notebook paper or on the back of my brother's homework assignments, that teach me to read between the lines. I become an interpreter of all things implied, a proficient reader of omission and nuance. A letter saying my father is catching up on his reading really says my father is slowing down, tiring easily. A cheerful note, written in pen on real stationery, makes me panic. It can only mean I am expected to believe everything is fine.

pacifica 1988

The summer days are cold and gray in Northern California. I live in a fog-bound two-room house near the ocean, built into the bending arms of Route 1. Living on another coast, in a different time zone, and yet my body defies science, never adjusting to the time difference. Everything feels off balance on this side of the continent. I wake early and comb the beach at sunrise. I fall asleep quickly after dinner, sometimes waking to find myself sitting on the couch, as if I never expected sleep to come.

On the cliffs surrounding the house farmers grow broccoli and brussels sprouts the size of small children. The morning breeze feels damp and carries the smell of aging vegetation and the sea. I keep the windows closed.

I visit the small fishing town where Hitchcock filmed *The Birds*. Sightseeing makes me feel like a visitor, an observer. One night I dream of the Great South Bay and my first swimming lesson. I am in the boat, having tossed my father in the water. I lean over, dangerously far, but cannot reach him. I wake up knowing before the phone rings that it's time to go home.

montauk 1988

At the farthest reaches of Long Island, where the fingertip of land stretches east into the Atlantic, we gather. My brothers in ill-fitting suits, no longer boys, but not quite men, their big hands and bulky wrists peeking out of suit jackets, their feet splayed in shiny shoes that reek of last-minute purchase. Here my mother holds the small urn of ashes. No pine box. No formal service. My mother's family does not attend. My father's family does not attend. Just immediate family. And we are immediate, getting up in the middle of the night when we get the call, to board planes and rent cars.

We make the long drive to the island's end together. The weather so cold that ice forms on the windshield as rain falls. Wiper fluid gone, my brother leans out the passenger-side window, reaching to clear the windshield with an old map. "This trip is going to kill us," my mother warns.

We park at the cliffs. Cold wind whips our hair. I watch my mother search the horizon like a lost child, my brothers standing close on either side. "So this is how a love story ends?" she asks.

We hold hands as the ashes swirl around our feet and calves. I let go and begin to swim where no sea runs, in the strong current of family that always pulls me in toward shore.

TRYST AND DOUBT

"So, let me get this straight," my sister, Stephanie, said when I tried to explain my no-strings-attached arrangement with my lover, Sam. "You've become the *other* other woman?" We were sitting at Captain Pete's Crab Shack, empty orange carcasses piled up between us.

"The intern's on the way out," I explained. "She's headed back to school, and he's moving back into his house, into the *guest room*." But even I couldn't fight the obviousness of the situation. "Yeah," I said, conceding. "Consider it the other woman, once removed."

Stephanie rolled her eyes. At thirty-three, she is the expert on men. She has a track record that's hard to beat with a list of ex-lovers that staggers the mind. This is because of the way she was raised; she had the inside scoop at a crucial time in her life and claims to know how men really think—which, she assures me, is quite different from the way women think.

I, on the other hand, am a dismal failure, dating married men and confirmed singles, falling in love at the first whiff of unavailability: If you're married, holding a torch for someone else, or are about to move out of town, here's my number, please call.

"Remember, what Sam doesn't know can't hurt him," Stephanie said, poking at me with a crab leg. "Hurt him now. While you still have the opportunity."

This is the type of wisdom she dispenses, the truth of the ages, handed down from woman to woman in an unbroken chain.

"You get what you ask for, Marie," she warned. Meaning, I suppose, that if I asked for nothing, that was exactly what I was going to get. Nothing.

"And that will be your future," she said. "Look closely."

The last time I saw my future, he was busy stuffing his ass into his pants, hopping on one foot searching for his other shoe.

"Out-of-town client," he said. "Delayed flight."

"You should have called her, Sam, left a message. She's not an idiot."

"Nope. I was busy working. By the time they arrived and the dinner meeting was over, it really was too late to call. How does that sound?"

"Like bullshit," I said. "Come back to bed for a few minutes."

"You're not a lot of help," he said as he unbuttoned his shirt.

The definition of karma is helping your lover come up with a good alibi for his wife about his late-night whereabouts and then having that same excuse used on you later. That's karma. But I wasn't thinking about karma when I met Sam. At the time, he was newly separated from his wife, sleeping on a couch in his office and in the process of ending an affair with an intern from work, a roller coaster of a summer fling that had left him tired and emotionally wrung out. "I'm not as young as I used to be, Marie," he said. He was forty-eight. "I'm not cut out for that kind of double life."

He told me all this in a confessional tone over drinks, while the intern was still in the picture, though fading on the horizon, and when he was thinking of moving back into his house because he missed living someplace with a permanent address, a firm support mattress, and a hot shower. There was something vulnerable in the way he told me his story, a healthy mix of humor, shame, and ego. I was instantly attracted. I was twenty-six, looking for a quiet place to lay my head. Nothing serious, we both agreed.

It's two in the morning when I arrive at Stephanie's front door. She doesn't seem surprised to see me. She leads me through the house to the kitchen, turns on the lights, and takes out two chilled glasses from the fridge. Her dark hair is piled high on her head, her movements brisk and efficient.

"You want me to help you—is that why you're here?" she asks, cutting lengthwise into a lime, preparing one of her famous gin and tonics.

"Lay it on me," I say. "The works." I tell her I want to know it all, how to read the signs and give the signals; I need some basic training when it comes to men.

The last time Stephanie and I lived together as family was over twenty years ago, and it was summer. Even though I was only five, I remember the sounds of that summer: the quiet ushering in of days, the steady rotation of the neighborhood sprinklers, my father sitting alone on our deck listening to a ballgame played in a distant city on a tiny radio no bigger than a child's hand.

One evening, sitting outside in the fading summer light, Stephanie laughed out loud at something, her mouth wide open, and she accidentally swallowed a firefly. I watched as she bit into the air, ensnaring it behind her teeth. I laughed then for no reason. I couldn't stop. I laughed while she gagged and gasped, stuck her tongue out and spit into her white T-shirt. She was quiet after that, her eyes wet from coughing. As the night grew dark around us, I began to see it: the slight light, soft and white around the edges, that seeped out from her pores.

I look at my sister now, in jean shorts and a red cropped T-shirt, standing barefoot in her kitchen making gin and tonics, and I am sure her lovers see it. On those nights when everything is still, when they reach out for her in a languid sleep, their fingertips touching the pillow where her head had just been, the light already fading, they must know. She has a glow, an aura that makes other women instinctively reach out and touch their lovers when she passes, a protective gesture to remind them of what is theirs. For even they know: It's not so difficult to have it all; the harder part is to keep it.

Stephanie reaches into the freezer for her secret ingredient—ice cubes made with tonic water—and fills the narrow glasses. "The problem with you, Marie, is that you're a romantic. You believe in happy endings."

"Is that so wrong?" I ask. "Is lesson number one called: Why Marie is crazy to think everything is going to work out alright?"

"No, it would be called: Common sense—how do I get some?" She bends beneath the counter for her stock of gin. "You're smart enough to know there's always something that goes beyond 'and they lived happily ever after.' That's never the end of the story."

"What makes you so sure?" I ask.

"What makes you so dense? Look at us, look at our parents."

I pull a stool close to the granite counter and watch Stephanie squeeze the juice from an overripe lime. I think about my mom pining away and my father's string of women. "If you mean we're doomed to repeat the same stupid mistakes as our parents, then shoot me now and put me out of my misery."

"It's like at the lake," she says, carefully measuring an even tablespoon of lime juice, her hands steady. "Remember that time when old Mrs. Rowen held her grandkid on her shoulder for hours while he slept? We all laughed when she walked around later with a hand outline on her back, and all the older women just smiled and nodded because they *knew* the deal."

"What deal? You're saying relationships are like tan lines— they're all going to fade over time? That's very deep."

"No. But they leave marks. We all have them. If you knew how to read them, you might have a clue about where you're headed, or see a little bit further down the road."

I press the cool glass against my cheek. Only my sister would think she has x-ray vision, capable of reading invisible scars that build up, crisscrossing and obscuring the heart. I empty my glass and hold it out for a refill. "I am obviously not drunk enough for this conversation."

When Stephanie was twelve and I was five, she went to live with my father, a separation that was not as seamless as it sounds. That was the summer I learned that people's lives are seldom as they appear, that there is a single moment in every day when things can turn around, a split second when decisions are made that can change the course of a life, the outcome of a marriage. It was in such a moment that my father walked out the door, taking my sister with him.

There are only two things I remember from the night my father left: the careful way he placed Stephanie's duffle bag into the trunk of the car, like tucking in a sleeping child, and the bright red eyes of the taillights as the car pulled away. My mother swears to this day she never saw it coming. After the dust settled and the lawyers were called off, that was pretty much how things played out, the battle lines drawn: I stayed with Mom, while Stephanie moved into an apartment with Dad in the city.

After our house divided, Stephanie and I would meet at rest stops on the New York State Thruway; my parents would park near each other and Stephanie and I would run out and switch cars—she would go with my mom for the weekend, I would go with my father—waving at each other as we passed. The rest stops were always the same cold concrete buildings with imposing vending machines that offered stale-looking food and scalding-hot beverages dispensed in Styrofoam cups. The only interesting thing was in the women's bathroom at one of them, where a shiny glass display case took up half a wall, housing sewing kits, comb-and-brush sets, bobby pins and hairnets, pink plastic curlers, and maxi pads in discrete white boxes with flowers on them. All the secrets of womanhood, revealed.

Stephanie once bought two small plastic Scottie dogs from the case, toys for desperate mothers looking for something to quiet and entertain the kids on those endless car rides between there and somewhere else. One was black, the other white, and they were glued to tiny magnets. Our parents were standing under a street lamp in a darkened parking lot, having a rare conversation. "Watch this," Stephanie said as she flipped over a greasy french fry container she'd fished from the trash. She placed one dog on top of the red-checkered box, the other below. The dog on top danced across the box by itself, spinning in easy circles and figure eights.

"How'd you do that?" I asked, reaching for the tiny dog. "Is it magic?"

"The power of opposites," she said, as if that explained everything. She gave me one of the dogs and placed the other in her pocket and we watched in silence as our parents finished their conversation in the small circular glow of light.

A few years later Stephanie decided she was too old to spend every other weekend with my mother, preferring to stay in the city with her friends or boyfriends, and then she went off to school. I guess I also became too old around the same time because once she stopped coming, my parents stopped meeting and I rarely saw her or my father at all.

"I just need to know some simple things," I said. "Can they be trained?"

Stephanie shrugged and added a second piece of lime to her drink. "You mean things like 'sit' and 'down boy'?"

"Sure," I said. "And don't forget 'stay.' That's always an important one."

"Well, I can work with you on 'sit'—and 'down boy' is especially useful—but 'stay' is a harder call; 'stay' is even beyond my power."

The legendary list of my sister's ex-lovers includes Sir Paws-a-Lot, the White Russian, Quick-Draw Magraw, the King of Pop, and good old Larry and Harry, a guy who insisted on calling his penis by name. Together they were a dynamic duo, though now I can't remember which was which. And that's just to name a few. She shed each of these men easily, moving on to the next and leaving behind a trail of unreturned phone calls, broken dates, and broken hearts: the detritus of relationships that have run their course.

"Tell me how you left it with Sam," she says. "Was it ugly?"

Only if you define ugly as the sound of keys grabbed quickly off the hall table; the lonely gait of a lover who favors his right leg when he trudges down the stairs; the hollow echo after the heavy front door has swung shut for the last time. But how do I explain this to Stephanie? Men don't leave her.

"Hand signals," I say. "Or the right look, or maybe even an invisible fence, the kind that sends out those tiny electric shock waves to discourage straying."

"You need to go to bed," she says. "We can talk about this in the morning."

"There's nothing like screwing up your life to make you feel like a grown-up," I say.

"That's why they call it adultery—emphasis on *adult*," she says. "Go to sleep."

"My next boyfriend is going to enjoy a good spanking." I say this as if I am imparting great wisdom.

"I didn't know you were into that."

"I'm not. It's just that a rolled-up newspaper across the bridge of the nose is not having the desired effect."

"I'll keep it in mind," she says.

"Never trust a man who tells you how much he loves his wife," I say. "That's the only advice I would give, if anyone around here were asking me. One minute they're talking about their homes and their cars, lulling you into a false sense of security, the next minute their hands are between your legs and you're kissing any hope of rational thought good-bye."

A dull headache and the sickening, acrid taste of lime are clear reminders of last night's conversation. I call Sam at the office and leave another message. He almost said he loved me once, letting it slip the last time we were in bed.

"What was that?" I'd asked. "Can you repeat that? I'm hard of hearing."

"Nothing," he'd said quickly, pulling the blanket up over my bare shoulder, tucking me in. "There are just things I love about you, that's all."

"Things?" I asked, now interested, more awake. In these moments the bed became our life raft; we were adrift, a swirling sea of darkness around us.

"Sure, I could reel off at least five things from the top of my head," he said.

Time spent with Sam had a stolen quality about it, existing only in the intersection of two very busy and different lives. "I don't know if that's such a good idea," I said.

"Why? Don't you think I can?" His voice had the tone of someone responding to a challenge. "I could name five good things right here and now. Besides, who doesn't want to hear something good?"

"We probably shouldn't get into this now." I rolled over, moving close to him. Lying close together, toes touching, we created our own tiny new country of two.

"Into what?" He put his arm around my shoulder. "I'm not trying to get into anything here."

"You know how it goes," I said. "Once you make a list of all the good things, then you automatically start thinking about all the bad things; that's how things like this work."

Sam didn't understand; he just wanted to name his five good things, right there on the spot. "What are you talking about? What are 'things like this'?"

"It's human nature," I said, trying to explain. "You can't fight it. You start with the good things and then *wham*!—you go right to the bad stuff. That's how it goes."

Sam pulled over his share of the covers. He said he was going to recite his list, whether I wanted to hear it or not. He said he loved that I was dependable, that I would be there when he called, that I had the most expressive eyes he had ever seen, and that he loved the way I walked, long, even strides he could watch forever.

"What do you think about that?" he said, pleased with himself, happy to prove he wasn't heading anywhere else: He could just name good things and brave the consequences, thumbing his nose at human nature.

His smile faded when I told him he only listed four things and the worst part was that he made me sound like a goddamned golden retriever. "All you left out was loyal."

I reached over and lit a cigarette. I was usually pretty careful about smoking or wearing heavy perfume around him, not wanting to send him home to his wife smelling like me—though I could always still smell him, on my clothes, my skin, long after we had parted.

"Four things," I said, holding out four fingers. "All of which made me sound like man's best friend."

He seemed shocked that I could criticize his list. "You think it's so easy? I'd like to see you try. Let's hear your list."

I didn't want to try and I could tell by the look on his face that he was hurt. I tried to explain to him that my mind didn't work that way, that I didn't think about things in terms of lists. I moved in a little closer to him and wrapped my legs around his. "Maybe we could practice some nonverbal communication," I whispered in his ear.

"Not even one good thing?" He untangled himself and got out of bed. I watched as he ran his foot along the edge of the futon mattress, trying to retrieve a discarded sock. "You can't even think of one good goddamned thing."

His shadow flickered behind him as he stood in front of the desk lamp, making him appear larger than life and blurry around the edges. He reached for his clothes, shapes disappearing into the dark wall. It was late, he said, he had to go. A heavy feeling settled in around my chest, a cold breeze blowing a door shut. I knew then, as he walked away from my apartment, there would be another list, an itemized recounting of all the bad things, a list that would grow and gain momentum with every step as he walked away.

"Salsa is not a breakfast food," I tell Stephanie as I take out a pitcher of cold water from the fridge.

"It is when it has mango in it," she says. "Try some."

The thought of food makes my stomach lurch. I pick up the phone and check voicemail. Nothing. "Tell me something," I say, hanging up the phone. "How do you keep from being the person who loves more?"

Stephanie is sitting at the kitchen table, legs crossed underneath her, flipping through the paper. The sunlight, far too bright and optimistic, leaks in around her. "Love isn't equal," she says, putting down the paper. "There is always one person who feels more, or needs more of something—security, reassurance, acceptance, whatever."

I pour water into my glass, taking a moment to respond. "Do you think that was Mom's problem? Do you think that's why she never realized Dad was going to leave?"

"Love had officially left the building," she says. "He was already gone."

There is a strong aroma of coffee in the room, a rich, dark brew courtesy of Stephanie's French press that reminds me of my father. He was a committed coffee drinker, grinding his own beans, ordering special imported blends. His gleaming silver coffeepot sat on the counter after he left, unused, until it was replaced by an electric juicer and then later a fat orange Crock-Pot. The smell of coffee catches in the back of my throat, an earthy smell that somehow reminds me of everything I've lost.

"Sam has great hands," I say. "I loved the feel of them against my skin."

"How's the headache?" Stephanie gets up from the table and pulls open a cabinet drawer. "Are we talking simple pain relief or do you need something with a little bit more kick?" She takes out three bottles of pills and lines them up along the counter. I watch as she opens the middle bottle, puts two tablets on her tongue, and tilts her chin to the ceiling, her neck pale and slender.

"And teeth, white but not perfectly straight. He has this great crooked smile." I am not sure at this point that it's even Sam I'm missing—maybe it's the ways of men, or the feel of a man in the house, something I was too young to remember fully. Instead I am left with the blurry, ragged edges encircling the hole in my life where my father once lived.

"You're obsessing," she says. "I hope you haven't told Sam any of this stuff. It's better to hold a little something back, don't show your hand; it's better to keep him guessing."

She is standing by the sink, rinsing out her glass. The windows above the sink are bright squares of light. Small particles of dust swim by. Stephanie is wearing only a long white T-shirt that skims the tops of her thighs. I can see the outline of her body in the sunlight, bending and moving with an easy grace. She looks like an illustration straight out of the one book we shared as children, about ancient gods and goddesses: Diana the huntress. I imagine the blue-veined wonder of her heart, whole and unblemished, beating out a simple pattern in a steady hush-hush rhythm. My head feels light, like it could float away, carried off like ash in the wind. "I didn't even tell him one good thing," I say. "He asked but I didn't say a word."

"Good," she says. "You're learning. That's a very good start."

Package Deal

The first time my father lies to me is on the day he comes home from the hospital and tells me he's going to be fine. "Really," he says. "Nothing to worry about." I cut school that day, staying home to make sure everything is perfect and ready—sheets turned down, pillows flipped to the cool side, magazines and TV remote handy, and a big pot of soup simmering on the stove, cooking down to nothing.

"You've got to stop with the death watch, Josie," is all my father says when he sees the newly cleaned house, orderly kitchen, and the shades at half mast in his bedroom. He pulls the belt of his robe a little tighter and shoves an extra blanket off the edge of the bed. "I'm alright," he says. "Believe me."

I don't believe him. Especially after my boyfriend, Danny, shows me what happened, rolling his eyes up in the back of his head, clutching and clawing at his chest, shaking. "It was scary as shit," Danny says, picking himself up from the ground. "You should have been here."

Danny and my father were playing chess the night it happened—Danny's been trying to learn the Dutch Stonewall Defense for weeks. "He's never going to make it as a player," my father said, calling out to me as I was leaving. "Can't think more than a few moves ahead. Not like you; you always knew when the other shoe was about to fall." I laughed, left them playing at the kitchen table, my father's glasses slipping down the bridge of his nose, Danny's head bowed in concentration. I didn't even turn back to look. That's how disaster happens, on a normal Thursday night: It sneaks in without warning while you're at the grocery store stocking up on Pop-Tarts and frozen pizzas for the weekend. By the time I got home the ambulance was already pulling away; I passed it on the block and didn't even realize it was coming from my own house.

This is not the first time I think my father is dying, but it might be the first time it's true. Two heart attacks before this one—or *episodes*, as my father called them—but this is the one that left its mark, a long, angry incision, where gloved hands broke his ribs and reached inside to touch his beating heart. We sit together now in the late afternoons and watch old TV shows, ones with canned laughter and happy resolutions. "You don't need to be inside taking care of an old man," he says. "Go out, get some fresh air."

"Fresh air? What am I, a puppy? I'm not going anywhere," I say, fluffing up his pillow. "I want to be around just in case."

"In case of what? Stop being so dramatic." He waves me away. "Shouldn't you be in school?"

"Don't worry about school, Harry," I say. "It's senior year. No big deal. Just lots of filler to keep us busy till we're out of there."

He doesn't seem to have the energy to give me a hard time. And when the school finally calls about my absences, he covers for me. "Mono," he says with a heavy sigh. "She may be out for a while."

I call my father Harry because that's his name. We're not the kind of family to get hung up on titles. Harry is not a young man; he's not even a middle-aged one. He was twenty-five years older than my mom when they married, in his mid-fifties when I was born. I've always been aware of his age, thought about how he was much older than my friends' parents, or cringed when people mistook him for my grandfather, but here is the thing: He outlived my mother. She died when I was eight. "It wasn't supposed to happen that way," he always said, as if trying to make sense of it himself. "I should have been the one to go first."

We live in a quiet commuter neighborhood, not far from the city, with orderly lawns and sensible floor plans. Totally average. Danny, my boyfriend, lives with us too. Some of the teachers at our school find that surprising. We don't. We're both seniors at Kennedy, and when Danny's dad got a chance at the London office, he took it. His parents thought it would be better for Danny to stay with us and finish his last year of school in the States. In the two years we've been seeing each other, this is probably the first time they've even thought about what would be best for Danny. I am not sure they were ever home long enough to notice that Danny had been practically living with us anyway.

At my house, Harry is always home. He used to be a trial lawyer once, but when my mom got sick he stayed home to take care of her and then when she died, he just didn't have the heart to go back. But don't get the idea that he's any kind of house husband or über dad; he's always forgetting to pick me up at soccer games or school dances, he always loses those parental consent forms, and he's not all that big on cooking and cleaning—nature is not the only thing that abhors a vacuum at our house.

It was Danny's idea not to tell anyone about what happened to Harry. He was worried his parents might get wind of it and have some crazy ideas about sending him away, making him go live with his great aunt in Philadelphia. I agreed, and the whole time Harry was in the hospital, we were careful to avoid attention from well-meaning neighbors or teachers who might have something to say about us living together without adult supervision. We were model students, arriving at school on time, coming straight home, doing our homework, taking turns putting dinner on the table by six thirty—frozen fried chicken, tater tots, canned string beans, tall glasses of milk—and cleaning up. Then it was strictly lights out by eleven, when we would fall asleep together, curled up under my old pink comforter.

When Harry finally did come home from the hospital, Danny and I were shocked by the way he looked—he had shrunk, gotten a size or two smaller in the wash. I mean, everything was still there, in the same place, but somehow it was smaller. Harry was never a tall man—five feet eight on a good day—but he always had the illusion of height. "You don't need lifts in your shoes; just carry it in your shoulders," he always said. "From the neck up, I'm a giant." Looking at him, on that first day home, he was no giant; it was like one of those Russian nesting dolls, the larger one replaced by its tinier version, the smaller one hidden inside all along, just waiting to get out.

"What are we going to do?" I ask Danny after Harry's return. We're sitting outside on the front steps in the fading light, talking in the serious low voices we've started using lately.

"We're going to do what we've been doing," Danny says, in that way of his that reduces things to their simplest form.

"College?" I ask. "Have you even thought about it lately? Don't we need to start making some plans or something?"

"No," he says. "Your dad's sick; he could use our help around here. What's the big deal?"

I look up at Harry's window, at the blue television shadows dancing against the walls. Before he got sick Harry always called TV the idiot box, acting like it was a mortal sin if you even turned it on during daylight hours. Now, he spends entire days in his room, watching the small television we moved in there.

"No big deal," I say. "I just thought one of us should be thinking about the future, that's all."

Wheel of Fortune comes on between a sleazy talk show and a soap opera. It's part of my morning routine with Harry, who likes to watch the show with the sound off and the radio on. He solves the puzzles faster than I do, with only a letter or two

on the screen, calling out the answers in a voice that carries—
"Bride of Frankenstein," "Flagstaff, Arizona," "Theodore Roosevelt"—while Mahler or Schumann plays in the background.

Harry's voice is just about the only thing that hasn't changed; it's still strong and clear as ever. As a kid, Harry had a bad stutter and was afraid to speak in public. He claims Cicero changed his life; he actually cured his own stutter by reading out loud with marbles in his mouth, the way Cicero once did with rocks. A lifetime later, when I struggled with tenth-grade Latin homework, he would walk over and easily spot-translate: "Cicero presents irrefutable evidence and forceful witness," even though it had been over fifty years since he looked at the stuff. I can tell you, fifty years from now, I will not remember how many parts Gaul had when Caesar was done with it.

"Looks like Vanna got a haircut," I say to Harry as I settle down next to him to watch TV.

"Didn't notice," he says. "I think she's involved with the short guy."

"Sajak? You've got to be kidding."

"They exchange a lot of looks. Very telling."

"You didn't notice the haircut, but you're interpreting looks?"

"What else have I got to do?" he asks, nodding toward the screen. "Watch her face when she looks over at him. It's all in the eyes."

"You're nuts," I say. "Did you take your pills yet?"

He shakes his head. "You're beginning to remind me a little of your mother, you know that?"

He has never said this before. When I think of my mother, she looks the way she did in my fifth birthday picture: a tall, pretty blonde in a pale-blue dress, smiling. Nothing like me—I am short and dark, and even though I will be eighteen in June, people always think I'm younger. Harry says I come from good peasant stock, my coloring and build a throwback to his side of the family.

"How?" I ask. "How am I like her?"

"The way you worry," he says. "You're always worried about me, just like she was—even at the end when she was really sick, she was more concerned about me or you than herself."

"Tell me something about her," I say. "Anything."

Harry sinks back into his bed and lays his palms flat against the quilt. "You know all the stories," he says. "No use in going back there."

"Tell me something I don't know, something about when you first met her, when you fell in love."

"Love, you want to hear about love?" Harry smiles, one of the first smiles I've seen in weeks. "Your mother was a practical woman. She had a way of looking at the world that was straightforward, no-nonsense. She was that way about love. Back when we first started dating, I used to think we were such an unconventional couple, you know, because I was so much older than she was. I used to wonder if other people would look at us and think: Why was that beautiful young woman hanging around with that old man? Your mother laughed when I told her that. She said, 'There's nothing unconventional about love, Harry; it's the oldest story in the book.'"

Danny brings home news from our friends: Buffalo, Syracuse, Hamilton. Everyone is leaving. Catalogs and applications pile up on the hall table but I don't look at them. I stop going to school almost entirely, though Danny makes an effort most mornings to encourage me to go, trying to wake me and get me to school. "The truant office called, they're on their way over—better get out of bed."

Days when Harry has his rounds of doctor's visits or rehabilitation therapy, I manage to get up in time and dress and go with him, hurrying to sit in waiting rooms all over town.

Sheila, the nurse at the cardiologist's office, saves me the good magazines on the days she knows I am coming in.

"Not a *Modern Maturity* or *Guideposts* in sight," she says, handing me a pile of celebrity tabloids. "How's the high school treating you? Old Cross-eyed Christy still working the front desk?"

"Still there," I say. "It's weird with everyone going away."

"It's getting to be that time," she says. "That's what happens."

"I'm worried about Harry," I say, blurting it out for the first time.

She looks down at my father's chart. "I can understand that," she says, nodding her head slowly. "I can totally understand."

At home I talk to Danny again about college. He's really into computers and plans on working with a few friends writing software when we finish school. He wants to stay here and help out, to live here with me and Harry. I don't exactly have a plan; I am not so sure I will even graduate, with all the school days I've missed. When Danny's near-perfect SAT scores arrive at the house, he acts like he doesn't care, that it doesn't matter, even when they attract attention and a few phone calls from colleges from around the country.

"Jim called again today," Harry tells us over dinner; it's the first time he's joined us at the table in more than a month. It seems strange to see him sitting with us again. Danny doesn't seem all that happy that Harry is on a first-name basis with the admissions guy from Boston College. "He thinks you have an excellent shot. Why not take the bus up to Boston this weekend and check it out for yourself?"

"Why would I want to do that?" Danny asks. "I don't want to go to Boston."

"It's a nice city," says Harry. "Very historic. You should see it at least once in your life."

"I don't see what the big deal is," Danny says. We're sitting outside on the steps after dinner, the cold air turning his cheeks red. "I don't want to go to college. I don't see the reason we have to go away." He is not giving up easily.

"Well, maybe we could just take a little ride up to Boston," I say. "It would be fun to get away, even for the weekend, to go look at the place."

"It probably just looks like a big school," Danny says. "If you have such a sudden interest in school, why don't you try visiting ours for a change?"

Saturday morning Harry joins us at breakfast. He seems excited, in a way I haven't seen him in months. "I'm expecting a phone call," he says mysteriously. Harry only uses the kitchen phone, the one with the short black cord. He won't even hear of replacing it with the cordless kind. "When I'm on the phone, I'm on the phone," he says. "I don't need to be up walking around." He has his yellow legal pad out and a few sharpened pencils at the ready.

Danny and I exchange puzzled looks and I shake my head. I have no idea what's going on. Danny keeps eating his Rice Krispies and barely looks up when the phone rings. I listen and watch Harry while he's on the phone, the way he jots down notes quickly and nods when he speaks, even though the person on the other end can't see him. He ends the call by saying, "Thanks for doing business on a Saturday, Bob. We'll get back in touch with you."

"What was that all about?" I ask.

"Listen," he says, turning back to us. "I've got you a deal. But first, let me ask you a question: How do you feel about Texas?"

Danny looks at me, confused.

Harry talks to me first, knowing that whatever is about to happen here is going to rest with me. "Texas A&M, ever heard of them?"

I shake my head.

"Well, you're about to." He actually chuckles here, like he's in on his own private joke. "Dan, they've offered you the whole deal, the free ride; a geology scholarship."

Danny looks shocked.

"And for you"—he points at me now—"they'll look the other way when it comes to your mediocre grades and spotty attendance; they're even willing to make you an automatic resident, giving you in-state tuition. In-state! Can you believe it? You know what they pay in Texas? Nothing. Less than nothing. I got you two a package deal. What do you say to that?"

We're too stunned to answer.

"I told the guy last week you come as a pair. They want him they've gotta accept you"—he points at me again—"or no dice."

That's it; in one swift move I have been relieved from death watch, and we've both been sent packing.

Dan seems crushed. "Geology? You want me to go away and study rocks?"

"Who knows what the hell it's about," says Harry, and brushes his hand away to dismiss the question. "It's Texas. I'm sure there's some oil involved. And rocks. Who cares. Get in, change your major later. I did this for you. It's the perfect deal for you both."

My father looks confused that we're not happy; he turns his head slowly from me to Danny. "What is this?" he asks. "What's with you guys?"

Danny announces loudly that he's not going—"No way!"—and storms away from the table, acting like the teenager he is.

"But I made you a deal," my father says again. I follow Danny out of the room, trying to catch up with him.

On the map Texas looks bigger than New York and about a half a country away. I imagine a supersized landscape, filled with cattle and men in cowboy hats and boots, and land that is flat and wide-open as a promise. The kind of place where you could be anyone you wanted to be, where simple words like *father* and *daughter* are pronounced with a strange new accent that makes everything sound like a song.

"So, a Texan is on this cruise to Alaska, and the whole time he's talking about how much bigger and better everything is back home, when along comes a huge iceberg into view."

"No more," Danny says, turning away from me on the bed to face the wall. "Enough about Texas, please."

"'Hell,' says the Texan, 'I've got to admit, you do got some big ice cubes here.'"

Danny groans, rolls over on the bed and stares at the ceiling. "That's not even funny."

"Go talk to him," I say. "He's hurt you weren't happy with his deal."

"Are you happy with it? I don't understand why he wants to get rid of us like that. You'd think he'd want us to stay in his condition—especially *you*. Did he really think we'd want to just leave and go to Texas?"

My Cinderella nightlight casts wavy yellow outlines of us on the ceiling; I raise my arm up and down a few times, watching as my shadow follows blindly along, never worried about being lost or left behind. Danny rolls over again to face the wall. I curl up tightly next to him.

"Do you know what the opposite of 'woe' is in Texas?" I ask. Danny sighs and doesn't answer. I lean in close and whisper in his ear. "Giddyup."

The letter sits on the hall table for almost a full week before I notice it. A thick white envelope, official-looking, addressed to me. It's from a local private college, one I'd forgotten I had even applied to months ago, before Harry's hospital trip. Danny must have brought it in, felt the heft, and known that a thick envelope could only mean one thing, yet he never mentioned it; he never said a word.

It's the kind of college that has its own stable and TV station, a place where all freshmen live on campus. There are green rolling hills and red brick buildings with white porches. Harry wears his courtroom best, a blue suit that hangs on him now, with fine white pinstripes, and a red tie with blue stripes. Danny drives as Harry gives directions, and I sit in the back, slightly nauseous.

The girls I meet could be fresh from a Ralph Lauren ad, all tall with straight hair and teeth, dressed in outfits that appear color-coordinated and well thought-out. I am wearing old jeans, a long-sleeved gray T-shirt, and a necklace that doubles as a hair band. I vaguely remember my application. It seems like years ago that I thought of this place as a safety school, and now it may be the only place that will take me if I agree to spend the entire summer in summer school. A lifetime ago I put down "classics" as my major. As I meet the faculty—almost everyone in the department is over sixty, like my father—and view the dorms, all single beds and single sex, I feel overwhelmed.

Harry tells me the place looks like a country club, a nice place to spend time. I can tell he's trying to make me feel better. Danny says nothing but he looks a little sick.

I send in my deposit and secure my place in the graduating class four years away. I stop sleeping, stop eating, don't even attempt to go to school, figuring I will make it all up in summer session.

At night I lie in bed and listen to Harry pace the upstairs hallways above my head. It's like the old days, when he would never sleep more than a few hours a night; I take it as a sign he's feeling better.

I find him in the kitchen. The small light over the sink is on and he's sitting at the table, eating a frozen chocolate cream pie straight from the box. He's got my old algebra book out and he's doing word problems on the back of a brown paper grocery bag.

"You shouldn't be eating that," I say.

He barely looks up. "You should be sleeping," he says. "What are you doing up?"

I take a fork from the drawer and join him. "I've got a lot of *angst*," I tell him. It's the first time I've used this word out loud.

"Yeah," he says, "me too. So what else is new."

"Look," I say. "This has been impossible. You've got to make us a deal. Find us somewhere else to go."

"I found you Texas; you weren't interested." He goes back to the pie. "Besides, it's too late now. The slots are filled, the big money is all given out."

"You know how dry it is in Texas?" I ask.

"Is this another one of your jokes?"

"The cows give evaporated milk."

"I can't get you another deal."

"The trees are whistling for dogs."

"It's not going to work," Harry says. "You can go to school nearby. He can do whatever he wants. His parents might actually have a few ideas for him."

"And that's that? I thought there was always a way, always some strategy still left to play; you're not giving up, are you?"

"What about you?" he asks. "Do you want to stay?"

I bite into the frozen chocolate pie, feel it dissolve in my mouth. "This place is killing me," I say. "I'm dying here."

"Join the club," he says. Then he looks up at me and our eyes meet. "I'll see what I can do."

We are co-conspirators. Harry decides Danny should go to City College; it's close and he can live at home. I write the essay, trying to sound young, enthusiastic, and hopeful, all the things I am not. Harry makes the right phone calls. Within two weeks, Danny is on the waitlist.

I break the news to Danny gently. We are sitting in my room on the floor. I tell him about the hour commute, how he can live at home with Harry, if he wants.

"What about you?" he asks. "Will you stay here with us?"

For some reason, we haven't talked about this before. It's like we started holding our breath when Harry came home and never remembered to let it out. We haven't talked about what comes after, how we go from living together to seeing each other over winter break and summer holidays. Our friends are leaving; I am worried about Harry, that he's not going to be around much longer, and that Danny and I will never be together in the same way. My heart feels heavy in my chest, weighing me down in this spot and I know if I don't go now, I will never be able to leave.

"Out," I say. "I really need to get out of here."

I can feel the pressure of his hand on my shoulder and I know he wants nothing, not one single thing to change from the way it is now, but everything around us is changing; there is nothing we can do about it. I can hear Harry's footsteps echoing in the upstairs hallway. I know that no matter how far away I go, I will always hear them.

I take Danny's hand. "Tell me about that one." I run my fingers along the edges of a sunburst mark on the back of Danny's hand.

"You already know this story," he says. "Cigarette burn."

"Accident?" I ask.

"Kind of. Courtesy of a drunken uncle caught up in ringing in the New Year. It happened years ago, when I was a kid."

I roll up my pant leg over my knee. Danny leans in close, brushes his lips against my knee.

"That one always looks like a crooked smile to me," he says. "A little secret grin."

"And here," I say, holding up my left hand. "Don't forget this one, across the knuckle."

Danny kisses the back of my hand, runs his tongue across the knuckle. "Tastes salty," he says, "like the ocean."

"That's because it happened at the beach. A piece of broken glass. My mom was still alive then. She bandaged it, but the bleeding wouldn't stop. She wanted to take me to the hospital for stitches but Harry told her it would be fine."

It's the first time I've thought about my mother in a while, when the three of us were together, the way we once belonged. Nothing feels worse than to suddenly remember someone you thought you'd never forget.

I unbutton my shirt and place Danny's hand against my chest. "And here," I say. "Don't forget this one."

Danny runs his fingers down my neck, pushing my shirt away. "I don't even remember this one," he says, nuzzling into my collarbone. "There's nothing here."

"Well, look closer," I say. "That's the tricky thing about scars. You never know where they're going to show up."

A few days later Harry greets us at the breakfast table, dressed in his suit again and smelling like the Old Spice soap-on-a-rope I gave him for Father's Day. There is a spring in his step; he even looks a little taller, and like what might almost pass for happy. A small private engineering school called, he tells us, in Jersey. "They're interested in Danny," he says. "I thought we might all go and take a look." He gives me a little wink.

"What about City College?" Danny asks.

"Well, this one is just as close," he says. "About an hour. You could come home on weekends, if you wanted. By the way, there's a train from there into the city." He looks at me. "Doesn't that school of yours have a satellite campus downtown? Of course, that one is mostly for business majors. You might have to get in and change your major later."

He holds the keys out, offering me the chance to drive.

"Jersey? You know what they say about driving in Jersey?" I take the keys from Harry. "The faster you go through a red light, the smaller the chance you have of getting hit."

"Get in the car, Jo," Harry says, sinking into the backseat as Danny and I sit up front. "Wake me when we cross the state line." He shuts his eyes, tired from the short walk to the car. "I'll give you the rest of the directions from there."

II

TRUE CONFESSIONS OF A BREAD BAKER

When I am nine years old I find the yellowed newspaper clippings. They are all of well publicized divorce trials featuring mob men and showgirls. The men—with nicknames like Leo the Leech or Benny the Bull—are pictured full-faced; the women, with their 48-hour figures spilling out of 24-hour undergarments, are shown to their best advantage, in profile. The divorce lawyer, always mentioned in the first paragraph, is my father. Some of the papers that chronicle these trials no longer exist: the *New York Globe* and *Daily Mirror*. The clippings are from before my birth.

These articles spark the idea of writing my own stories, tales of a nine-year-old girl with a lawyer father and scandalous clients. Nancy Drew, eat your heart out: This is no milquetoast lawyer dad like Carson Drew, but rather my lurid retelling of public scandal, sensationalist angles, and sex—or what passes for sex when you're nine.

I proudly show these stories to my father, who, when he reads them, shakes his head and tells me: "You're funny, kid, but don't write what you know." I realize this means he doesn't want me to write about him.

At twelve my parents exchange their city apartment for a house in the country and we get a different view of the Hudson. It is the year I learn the meaning of the word "disbarred." Because of this unplanned midyear move and a lousy public school system, I find myself the only Jew at Sacred Heart Middle School, an all-girl affair that is terrifying at every turn. After my first day of school I tell my father about the life-sized, half-naked man nailed up in the entranceway. "That's what they do to Jews who get a big head," he tells me. "Watch yourself."

At the height of this preadolescent angst I get the idea to write to Woody Allen. After all, who better to relate to my sense of feeling out of place? I have just seen *Annie Hall* and I am convinced Woody will understand. I write to him about my recent exile from the city, my parochial school experience, the works. I even send along a picture of me in full *Annie Hall* regalia, wearing my father's tie and vest and a hat I bought at a church bazaar, for good measure.

"You're just a young girl," everybody says. "Why would he write back to you?"

Two weeks later there is a handwritten reply from an Upper West Side address—of course he's always happy to hear from a fan! Have I read Kafka? Have I seen Bergman? This is decades before movies on demand; I have no prayer of seeing Bergman. The movie theater in my town has been running *The Sound of Music* for about six weeks straight. I read Kafka and write an in-depth analysis—"I think he's very funny." Woody writes not to worry about Bergman, that he would be happy to take me to a movie when I come to the city. He also tells me about a film he is making with another twelve-year-old girl, Mariel Hemingway. We correspond for a while and I decide I can trust him with my stories, romantic tales of a twelve-year-old girl who has a famous movie director as a pen pal. I receive his last note after I send those stories, a postcard from L.A. On it Woody writes: "You're funny, kid, but don't write what you know." I realize this means he doesn't want me to write about him.

At twenty-five I am four years older than my lover's daughter. My lover is a poet who studied at Kenyon at the slippered feet of John Crowe Ransom, and with a cranky Robert Frost. After Kenyon, he went on to divinity school in New Haven. He can actually marry people in the state of Connecticut. Maybe that's why the whole time we're living together we never leave New York.

We break up over Mexican on Bleecker Street. In the background there is a roving mariachi band, moving stealthily from table to table. Behind us a group of NYU frat boys, who think they recognize the "Frito Bandito" song, start singing. While I am trying to listen to words that make no sense—"Timing, not working out, you're too young"—the boys chant *aye yi yi yi* in the background, like some kind of crazed Greek chorus.

During this, our last conversation, our last meal over Mexican, my lover confesses to *accidentally* finding my journal, one I placed behind a bag of potting soil under some cleaning supplies in back of the utility closet. My journal is filled with stories of a young girl who lives with a narcissistic poet in an undersized apartment in New York. One of the last things my lover says to me as he gets up to leave the table is: "You're funny, kid, but don't write what you know." I realize this means he doesn't want me to write about him.

So, now I am thirty and living with a scientist who plays the piano, translates French literature for fun, and teaches me to bake bread—warm yeasty loaves that sit on the kitchen counter in the house we share. I live on a street that doesn't run in cement blocks, with trees and lawns and homes with more than one room. And I begin to write again. This time, I write in the voice of first person witness—urban stories of single women, quirky narratives of young girls who love houseplants. The scientist reads these and says to me: "You're funny, but why don't you write what you know?" I realize this means he *wants* me to write about him. But by this time it's too late. I have learned to combine yeast, flour, water, and salt: the basic elements that ferment and bubble and bake into something that resembles none of its murky beginnings and yet tastes only like truth to the mouth.

Pressure System

A couple spends the week at the beach. It's humid and damp, the kind of place where sand gets into everything and everything feels moist; a place where book pages swell fat with water, where ink bleeds.

Their plan, unspoken, is to rekindle something, to recapture—what, they're not sure. But this is it—no electronic intrusions! No plush conveniences! The deprivation makes them feel giddy and light, happy to be free from the divisive distractions of daily life. A week to revisit themselves as a couple, alone.

Only a day at the house and she begins to complain that her hair has gained weight. Seriously, she says, it's plumping out at the shaft—it's retaining water. She moves slowly from room to room, her limbs soft and languid, her hair full from humidity. She claims she can feel the air, its soggy resistance pressing against her. Oppressive, she says often, even when nobody is listening. She stays outside for only short periods, going out late in the day, avoiding sunlight, always seeking shade.

For him the pervasive dampness is a call to action. To combat it he falls into the habit of showering twice a day, sometimes more, although it never leaves him cool or refreshed. In the outdoor shower, with its cement floor and knotted pinewood walls, he sprays warm water against his damp skin and showers again and again, trying to fight off the feeling that he's sinking into some primordial ooze, something he can't escape. He spends a great part of his day indoors, wearing just a towel wrapped around his waist, a low-slung towel revealing a knob of hip bone. He always seems to be in some transient state, either just stepping into the shower or just stepping out.

And then the day comes, about midweek, when she has retreated to the room and is lying on the bed, the ceiling fan the only cooling source whirring above her as if it's cleared for take-off. She lies on her stomach, head hanging off the bed, reading a magazine that's open on the floor. Her stomach, flat again after a recent loss, presses hard against the itchy bedspread.

He walks by and sees her. He's wearing a towel, a loud checkered number that she has claimed will cause her to go blind or mad if she looks directly into it. Saying nothing, he walks into the room and sits next to her on the bed. On the dresser he sees a wooden black bristle hairbrush. He picks it up and begins to brush her hair, from scalp to end, methodically, over and over, until he creates a thick veil; a curtain of hair falling over her shoulders, over the side of the bed.

She turns her head then to face him. She pushes aside the curtain and braves blindness by staring directly into that crazy-checkered towel. In the background Sinatra on the radio, playing constantly on the one clear station since their arrival. The music a tribute or elegy to a different time.

He'll later say that hair brushing business wasn't the whole story. No way. In fact, for him the most memorable thing about the vacation was the storm. He is quick to remind her again of the night they spent holed up in the tiny beach shack with bottled water and candles and that dim-bulbed pink Minnie Mouse flashlight some kid left behind. And those winds, the ones that blew through the goddamned house—through it!— shook it silly on its high stilted perch, rattling the foundation, battering lawn furniture and scattering beach toys. Now *that* was a storm.

Of the storm she mostly remembers the stillness of the blackout, lying next to him in bed, the tiny radio no bigger than a child's hand placed between them—Sinatra had finally been put to rest, pushed aside for weather warnings, the red alert of a quickly changing pressure system. What she can't forget is the next day, the surreal brightness, the neighbor's missing cat found floating in the drainpipe, eyes wide open. And the beach, whole chunks of it gone, the reclamation of water and wind. That's what gets to her, the erosion and loss. It's the power of nature, he tells her. That's what it's all about.

He remembers the storm, she remembers the aftermath. And the complete story, the beach, the brush, the pressure front, and that crazy old towel, the one that made her fear she would go blind? Well, he'll tell you those things are all the same, really. And his hand will once again graze her thigh as she passes near. And she will smile over his shoulder when he holds her close. And they will agree. It's about those moments, the small spaces in the story, a pause that can break your heart, and the quiet scene, as quick as the downstroke of a brush, that can save you.

TALK

Your parents will talk to you as if you are a child. The fact that you are not a child does not matter. You are almost 30, living on your own in New York, and yet your voicemail is filled with their messages: File your taxes, write a thank-you note, call a cousin who just moved to the city. When you hear this: Skip through messages, sort old mail; doodle perfect circles one right after the other.

Your boyfriend will talk to you as if you are an idiot. The fact that you are not an idiot does not matter. He leaves sincere-sounding messages on your voicemail explaining: late-night meetings, last-minute excuses, a visiting female cousin. When you hear this: Roll your eyes; chew your pen cap; mimic his "sincere tones" out loud to yourself.

Your best friend will talk to you as if the world is made up of easy answers. The fact that the world, for you, is not made up of easy answers does not matter. At a local coffee shop you play the "you need" game: You need a new outfit, a new apartment, a new life. This week she tells you: "You need a new haircut— one that says 'fuck me.'" You think you would prefer one that says "fuck you." Raising your foot to a neighboring chair, you point to your black platform patents with toe cleavage and buckle strap and say: "My shoes already say 'fuck me.'" She mixes another pink-packaged sweetener into her double mochaccino and does not argue with your logic.

Your boss will talk to you as if you are a mind reader. The fact that you are not a mind reader does not matter. Most of her sentences begin: "Didn't you know...?" You didn't. When she speaks: Look at her blankly and try to remember something you never forgot. Nod your head and think of being somewhere else.

You work in Web design for a site dedicated to teen celebrity sightings and other gossip. You spend your days matching words—"smokin' hot," "sassy and sexy"—to images of young guys in tight T-shirts, boys with hair longer than yours. You make it a habit never to visit your own site.

Your boyfriend travels a lot. He sells airtime. The first time you met him you asked: "Whose air?" He held your face in his hands, laughed and never answered. When he is out of town, he will not call. Instead he'll text ambiguous messages, telling you his return date. Today you get one that says: *Friday!* With an exclamation point. When your girlfriend asks you when he is returning you say: "*Friday!*" You try to make the word sound like it comes with an exclamation point.

On *Friday!* you spend your lunch half-hour perusing magazines at a local kiosk. You are drawn to an expensive glossy gourmet number with large gold words on its cover: *Romantic French Dinners for Two.* You imagine the woman who works at this glossy is better paid than you. You can easily picture her: upscale office, cashmere sweater set, matching leather belt and shoes. You try not to think about your black leggings covered in cat hair and your sweatshirt that says *Bauhaus.* At her office, you are sure, there is classical music piped in; you know she spends her day amid words like "luscious" and "succulent."

Back at your office you flip through your new gourmet find. Classic rock is piped in from ambient speakers and you mouth the words to an old Stones tune while you make a shopping list for your *Romantic French Dinner for Two.* You tell a coworker you're making your boyfriend *poisson en meurette*, letting the *r*'s roll in the back of your throat like a gargle. She looks at you strangely and says: "You're making him poison?"

On the Q to Gristedes, somewhere in the neighborhood of West Fifty-seventh, the train stops, cutting its lights and motor. A man next to you, in a Burberry raincoat, rubs against your leg. You think of the old joke about how to get to Carnegie Hall; you know it is not on the Q train.

At Gristedes the can stacker looks like a young boy from your teen site. You tell him you are on a sole-search. He directs you to aisle three. He does not smile. You fill your hand-held basket with thyme, garlic, and sole and hum to the Muzak version of "You Can't Always Get What You Want."

At home you check your voicemail. You feel a tremor vibrating through you. You have just foraged for sole; you are not up to hearing excuses. The first word you hear is *Sweetheart.* You know this means trouble.

You decide getting drunk alone is a cliché and call your best friend. She is a cross between a golden retriever and the Pope—she will follow you anywhere and then forgive you. She will understand; she will tell you: "You need a new boyfriend, one who shows up." Unfortunately, she is not at home. Instead you leave her a message about the hazards of dating.

You begin to talk to yourself like a soothsayer—predicting your boyfriend will come crawling back on his knees, begging for you to understand, *just this once.* You know he will call within 24 hours to talk about miscommunication. Out loud you say: "He'll be sorry. He'll see. He'll fall all over himself trying to get me back."

Your cat rubs against your leg, smelling the fresh sole, ignoring your diatribe. You have read cats see only in monochrome. You remember your boyfriend is colorblind. In an early fight he laughed when you said: "You make me see red." You know he will never see red. Just as you know he will one day call someone else's machine and leave a message that begins: *Sweetheart.*

You wrap your arms across your shoulders and press them in close to your chest. You pace. There is a difference, you think, between falling out of love and falling apart. You begin to talk to yourself in a new way. Your tone is soothing. Gentle. At first this sure, quiet voice sounds strange, unrecognizable. But this is a beginning; it will take time: One day soon it will be the only voice you hear.

Good Advice

All it takes to get a man's attention is a fifty-nine-cent pair of plastic handcuffs and a see-through purse. Believe me, I know. I wrote the book. Yes, that's right, it's me, author of *Life Lessons from the Ladies' Room.* You're probably wondering, what is a bestselling author, a gal with "her finger on the pulse of the modern woman, who succinctly captures the zeitgeist of cultural concupiscence" (according to the *New York Newsday* Trends department) doing waiting around in a crappy paneled office with all the appeal of a low-rent watering hole that caters to dentists and podiatrists?

Media training.

I am here for formal sit-down sessions on how to walk, talk, and dress for public consumption. Not my idea, I assure you. They all laughed at first at my little off-the-record comment, a wink and nod and shoulder shrug, and we all thought it would pass. Publisher and agent both subscribing to the "Any ink shed is good ink" theory, as long as they get the book title right. That was then. Now they're not so sure, as visions of spiraling profits, merchandising pull-outs, and franchise deals going down in flames dance in their heads.

It really was off the record. How was I supposed to know that bitch from *Modern Woman* would quote me? It was a little slip of the lip, a nonsense comment and here I sit waiting to be taught the right way to speak, to present myself to the media, to prepare for talk show appearances, live interviews, radio call-in shows, and press tours. As the glossy brochures promise, when these highly polished professional trainers are done taking me through my paces, I will walk and talk like a winner, fully schooled in the three "P's" of Promotion: Preparation, Preparation, Preparation.

Unfortunately, I never did well in school. But never fear, because that's where Stork Lady and Little Boy come in with their professional smiles spread wide and long, cheek to cheek, while their eyes remain unsmiling and focused on me, looking for the tiniest detail to pick apart. They're here to spit-shine my image, not to be my friends, they explain; you've gotta crack a few eggs, says the Stork Lady, to make an omelet, right? They're actually getting paid hundreds of dollars an hour to say this kind of crap.

Bright lights, a desk made from fake wood, and a chair on wheels. All the comforts of home, laughs Little Boy as he leads me to the chair. His hands are small for a man, like starfish, and I like imagining him suddenly pulled out to sea.

Softball pitch first, explains Stork Lady. Her neck is long and pale and sways back and forth when she speaks; her eyes blink quickly behind thick lenses.

"How did you learn these life lessons?"

The lights are hot; I can feel the sweat starting to run down my spine. If this session ruins my new red silk shirt, someone is paying the dry cleaning bill and it sure as hell won't be me.

Such a typical question. Why doesn't anyone ever ask more interesting questions, like: How come everyone else doesn't know these things? But I guess I should just thank God they don't because there wouldn't be a six-figure book deal if they did.

"You don't need a degree in English to write a book about real life," I say, squinting into the lights. "All I needed to do was live it." I force a smile.

They both shake their heads. Stork Lady purses her lips. "Too defensive," says Little Boy. I need to try it again.

"I'm just observant," I say. "I write what I know."

Better. I guess it might seem obvious now, reading my book, that I write about things any woman should know *before* shelling out the bucks for my book—conveniently located at airports, grocery stores, and retail outlets, and newly released in special reference "pocket size!" edition. But still, I am grateful people need to be reminded of the simple things, the kind of things everyone should know, but for some reason they just don't.

The trainers nod their heads in unison, in that I-think-she-got-it kind of way, and I can tell it's going to be a long afternoon.

Blame the vagina. When that bitch from *New Woman* asked me to explain about lesson number fifteen—All women have ESP (a simple fact, if anyone ever bothered to think about it, which of course nobody does) and a built-in lie detector—I went ahead and quoted my mom: "Anyone with a twat knows which way the wind blows." Of course, I cleaned it up for the interviewer. I am not a total idiot; I said "vagina," not that

that high-polished twat appreciated my effort. It's not like I
gave anyone the helpful anecdote *behind* the ESP line, about
how my mother and I both knew when my little sister OD'd,
how I had the sad gloomies all day, just three personal gray
clouds hovering over my brain. About how when I walked
into the house and saw my mother sitting at the table in her
nightdress, looking vacantly off into space and smoking, I just
burst out crying and then she did the same. We were standing
in the kitchen, hugging each other and crying before we knew,
I mean *officially* knew, before the hospital called us from two
states away, before we had to drive all night to identify the
body in a hospital basement with walls the color of dried
mustard, we both just knew my baby sister was dead. Bad
news travels fast, people always say, but what they never tell
you is how it travels. I heard an explanation once about how
TV works, how images are broken down into particles and
sent out in waves of air. When you get right down to it, sadness
and bad news and loss all work the same way; tiny cloudy bits
are transmitted, as my mother always said, and anyone with
the right plumbing has no trouble picking up the reception.

"Lean forward," Little Boy instructs. "It will make it look
like you're more engaged."

They are filled with these helpful hints, treating me like
a child, taking me through these practice sessions again
and again. When they're done they will go back and write
up their report, let my publisher know if I am sufficiently
colorful or just too dangerous; it's a fine line between colorful

and dangerous, I am told, and apparently I skirt that line all the time. Say the wrong thing and sales could plummet, then fall off and then you've screwed the pooch—there goes the franchise, the T-shirts already selling at the mall (If you have to ask, you just don't get it—Life Lesson #8), the call-in show— my mother would have been thrilled; she always told me I had a face for radio—and the possible *Life Lessons* spin-offs geared toward teens. This is it, my moment, and if I sit back, let them primp and pose me, buy me clothes and make me practice sitting in sensible skirts with my legs closed, there just might be another zero tacked on at the end of the check at the end of the day.

"Tell us about your next project."

Another softball pitch. Feed me the easy lines and watch me mess up. They lean in, waiting for my response, shiny and bright with anticipation.

"A follow-up book," I say, trying to smile wide and toothy. "I'm thinking of calling this one *Life Sentences*."

"No, no," says Little Boy, his ears rising and falling a bit with each "no." "Don't use the word 'book'; it's far too limiting. Stick with 'project'. It's more open-ended."

"A follow-up *project*," I say, repeating the word after him.

One of the questions I am told to expect is about how I became the voice of universal truth for women. I should try to give some background, put a human face on my story with a few well-practiced anecdotes. These stories need to be light and breezy and appear off the cuff. And forget about humor, they tell me; it will only get me into trouble unless I learn how to deliver things in a tongue-in-cheek kind of way, "dry with a side of wry" they call it. I need to also practice my delivery.

I don't know about the delivery service. I am just the messenger, I tell them; these are the truths, and once you hear them you smack you head and nod, because what I say *is* true. You know it when you hear it. That's just how it goes.

"Oh, that is far too in-your-face," says Stork Lady, making a note on her clipboard. "We're going to have to work on that."

"Why don't you just tell us about your life," Little Boy suggests, rocking back on his well-polished heels. "Tell us some things about growing up. We'll take notes and sift through it all and find the good stuff. Go ahead."

I look at them blankly. They're going to package my story along with packaging me.

"The point is to create a winning story," says the Stork Lady. "Remember, your audience will care when you can connect with them."

She clicks off the supernova that was burning a hole in the back of my head and the regular fluorescent lights, the ones that normally give me a headache, are suddenly a relief and I feel as if I can truly exhale.

I remind them that I do connect with people, letting them know that my sales show that I don't even need to promote this anymore; people, especially women, get it, but that doesn't seem to be the point here. There's always room for *more*; for more television, radio, and personal appearances; for more road dates and readings and hotel rooms with scratchy bedspreads and headboards bolted to the wall. There's talk now that a prime-time newsmagazine owned by my book company is getting ready to cover the phenomena created by the book. So won't I just please practice and try to become more telegenic—remember: Don't wear red; it will bleed on camera—and learn how to give my "messages"—the main points on why people need to read my book. Give it the old college try, they actually say, when trying to appeal to me, even though I only attended one semester at my local community college when I was twenty, back when I had the idea I wanted to work with slow children, the ones who sit in the corners of the room, too locked inside their own heads to speak. Back when I used to want to help people when they are smaller versions of themselves, before they grow tall and hard.

"Helping people!" Little Boy practically jumps up and down with delight. "That's the message. Let's definitely capitalize on that one." He writes a quick note and I can see him circling it on the clipboard. This gives me a quick sinking feeling, as every time I try to help someone things usually have a way of going wrong.

What are you trying to teach people with your life lessons? This is practice question number three, right after why I felt "compelled" to write this. (Because I want to help people, right? Yes, they nod and tell me to keep going.) The third question, they want to brainstorm; I am told to free-associate, think about my ideas, the times I learned these lessons. I tell them about the time I was pushed down a flight of stairs by my grandfather and was unconscious for two whole days (It's okay to rest; you'll still wake up for the good parts—Life Lesson

#9) and about the time I was underage and drank a pitcher of margaritas and woke up naked on my neighbor's lawn (You can never be over-dressed—Life Lesson #22).

Apparently these are not exactly the types of stories they are looking for. I'm told to keep it simple, to go for a PG or G rating, try to think: general audiences. A newspaper recently did a story about my book, about how it's slipped into the language of everyday life. It's become a sort of shorthand or code among groups of women. There are even sororities where the girls can speak my numbers as a second language—Don't pull a #31 (Wishful thinking is bad for a relationship) or he's doing #36 (No matter how furtive or quick the glance, a woman always knows when a man is looking at her breasts).

The Stork Lady's hair never moves, even when her head bobs up and down during the "empathetic" re-enactment—I am supposed to look deeply into the eyes of the interviewer, nod my head slowly and purse my lips into a tight letter "o." Her hair is coifed and straight, a glossy helmet of perfection. Green room etiquette and personal grooming is also on the menu for today. Perming is out, straightening is in, the Stork informs me, fingering my curling twice-priced hair. "It's natural," I tell her. "I am just blessed." (Curly hair is not a blessing—Life Lesson #18.) I smile at my own joke. She nods, pulling a number eight, but her lips are thin and clearly she hasn't read my book because she would know I'm kidding. Iron, she says, we'll iron the curls right out of this, as if she has to tell an ethnic girl the secret of passing, about how to look like everyone else. I wrote the book, after all, didn't I?

Think in sound bites, I am told; practice your anecdotes. And so I do. A few lessons are sanctioned and I need to practice saying them out loud in front of a mirror: Avoid a woman who competes with her mother or her sister and embrace a woman who is best friends with either (#17); A small gift that shows you've been listening is worth twice the value of something larger that holds no meaning (#23); Household appliances and cleaning supplies are never appropriate gifts for wedding showers (#34); Accept or give an occasional love bite, but gnawing is out of the question (#47). The more brothers you have, the less chance you will find men mysterious or disgusting (#51).

They try to teach me. An uphill battle, I hear Stork whisper none too quietly. (If you want to be heard, whisper through your teeth while smiling—something I note for the next book, or project, or whatever...) So, I bide my time, and wait for the inevitable, for what I know is coming.

For me, I know it will all come back to number eighty-eight—the hotter the burn, the faster the burnout. "Meteoric" is the word used to describe my book in the press. Every time I hear it I know what it means. Meteors are what killed the dinosaurs, blanketed them in a thick, dark fog of smoke until they suffocated on their own weather conditions. And that's what's coming for me. Somewhere in the distance the other shoe is about to fall (#11) and when it does, when it comes, anything worth holding onto will slip and fall away with all the power and force of a penny dropped from a skyscraper. Gravity takes its toll (#53); I know there's just no arguing with nature. But for now I practice my smile, level my gaze and copy the correct head tilt. I will memorize my anecdotes and messages, work on my clothing choices and haircuts, even though I know it will make no difference. I am not the least bit concerned, as I am content in my knowledge that everything that rises has a downside and that nothing in this world is more satisfying than the word "comeback" (#96).

SIGNIFICANT OTHER

She has never thought of herself as the other-woman type. A woman who had a relationship with a married, unattainable man—who would ever want that? And yet, more and more, when women around her would casually mention certain key words—his wife, house, kids—she found herself paying close attention. She became a proficient eavesdropper, able to pick up nearby conversations in noisy restaurants where women were often found huddled deep in consultation about whether he would ever leave *her.*

He is over twenty years her senior. A man who moved easily in the world, unaware of his own appeal. He never passed anywhere near without her pulse springing to attention, its rapid staccato a visceral warning. She remained in a hyperaware state. Alert. When he asked her for their first date, an early dinner, she was ready.

She would think of this dinner as the first step. He would think of it as the event that changed everything. In his memory it happened this way:

They were seated across from each other at an interior table, away from the windows, the way he liked. The linen starched white between them, like a shroud. She was wearing a low-cut sleeveless dress the color of crushed grapes—it was a warm day in New York, a false start on spring. He made note of everything: her wispy fine hair, a faint smell of gardenias, sandals revealing a hint of cleavage between her toes. The restaurant was crowded, busy with the sounds of other dining patrons.

He talked. He told her of his work, his theories of life, home— even wife and kids (he couldn't stop himself). And she listened. She drank her wine, looked up at him with large dark eyes, propped her head up on a graceful hand, and listened. He found her an eager audience. As he talked he watched the way the dress clung to her body, pressed close against her full breasts. Beneath her dress she had nothing on, of that he could be fairly certain.

From restaurant to apartment. A studio sublet from a novelist away on a grant. There were books, pens, papers, a computer with a cover over it. The stuff of fiction. She closed the door and slid the bolt. It was in that simple act that it began. To him it was as if he were watching a movie: the dimmed lighting, a close-up on his shaky hands. Was he really going to do this? He felt he had finally, somehow, become a principal performer; this was a defining moment.

The apartment was small, one room. The walls were painted an enlightened green, the color of a skinned avocado. There were travel posters on the walls and photographs of rough-textured fruit. Next to him was a futon covered with a brightly colored afghan and to the left a small window was engulfed by a large gold picture frame.

"It looks like a festival in here," he said. The words tumbled from his mouth; they had no meaning.

As if without cause, she put her arm out toward him, touching the side of his face with her fingers. He knelt at her feet, holding her slim ankles, his hands clasped as if in prayer. She kneeled next to him, raising her arms, letting him lift the dress the color of crushed grapes from her body.

The low-slung futon mattress, the late sun shut out behind sharp vertical blinds—he was removing his own clothes, escaping. He drew her toward him, toward the bed. She lay down, waiting and silent. He averted his eyes, an acolyte, a true believer. His voice lost, he held tightly to her knees to keep from drowning in her newness.

Curiously, she remembers it differently, remembers spontaneity, equality, and, in the end, a sense of inevitability. She remembers asking: How did you like the festival? This does not mesh with his recollection and she does not argue the point. You would think a relationship developing under such highly charged auspices—his wife, split allegiances, the inherent drama of the situation—would have waged an emotional toll on its participants. But in this stage—if wed they would have been called newly marrieds; in an affair, newly coupled?—they found themselves renewed. She seemed to have more energy, though she was getting much less sleep. He was eager to leave for Grand Central in the morning, humming an old tune, one forgotten from youth. And the two of them, she and he, walking in step, a hurried pace to her apartment—all intensity and heat, part desire, part need. She saw the looks then, of other people. Envious. Knowing.

Spring, a late dusk, and they would fall into each other's arms, limbs tired, shaky. They lived in an insular world: the world of two. Time was always *now*, measured and meted out by how long they were to be apart, how briefly they were together. It was time felt by the body, delineated by the heart. (He had professed his love of her. And she had done the same.) And then: "I miss you, already" said while he stepped hurriedly into pants, tucking in the tails of his shirt with brisk movements. Miss you, she said. *Miss, missing, mistress.*

They thought they knew each other before that first day in her apartment, before that afternoon in her bed. All that early talk and more talk. The quandary, the constant litany in his head: Should I, should I, should I? And then the courting talk, the thrust and parry of conversation. And the stories: he reporting on the escapades of his pre-family days, of the young man he was. And she responding with funny, self-deprecating stories. Stories that made him see her in a charmed light, evoking a casual sweetness. Yes, he thought, this is what he wanted to tell her: Why didn't we meet earlier? Why only now when I am this tired, this married?

At the end of their first year together he offered to buy her a bed, one that was firm and supportive, something high off the ground. This was not what she had in mind. This was not moving forward, a progression of their love.

He stood in the middle of the small apartment. "Here," he said, gesturing with his hand. He pointed to the empty space below the window. "This is where the bed should go." He was wearing a white Oxford shirt that skimmed the tops of his bare thighs. She wore only his boxers, white with a red stripe. He wrapped his arms around her waist, turned her toward the window, toward the imaginary bed. "It'll be perfect," he said. She felt the way his arms wrapped tight around her. "Perfect," she said.

His children were ten and twelve that year. Difficult ages for his girls, he told her. She had seen the pictures, peeked into his wallet once when he was sleeping. They were carbon copies of their mother (also in the picture): same dark hair, same light eyes, and that knowing smile, somehow out of place on their young clean-scrubbed faces.

Not the time to make a decision, he said. Wait. She thought of women who grew bitter, who spent years waiting in empty beds. Thin, well-kept women always ready at the phone during odd, off hours, waiting for whispered calls made in haste. She began to think of all the expressions: assignation, tryst, affair. As if naming the act made it easier to classify, to understand. She thought Anna and Vronsky. And Emma and Leon. Sure they wrote books about these things, like it was only fiction— unhappy endings, all.

A stolen Saturday when he was to be at the office. Rain beating against thin panes, an afternoon in her new bed. After, she watched him walk to the window, able to see the back of his head and the reflection of his face. "You make me believe in possibilities," he'd told her once, a long time ago. She knew he meant: You make me feel young. She is reminded of this as she watches how the lines around his eyes deepen and furrow when he squints, when he comes face to face with himself at the window.

"Come back to bed," she told him. "It's half-empty without you."

He turned, looked down at her bare shoulders peeking out above the afghan.

"Funny," he said. "I thought it was half-full."

Then a break in the weather, a walk hand-in-hand to Central Park. The zoo, the photo machine, the four neatly stacked pictures, his hands and arms blurry, reaching out toward the edge of the frame, frozen in motion.

～

Then one day, on the other side of fifty, he begins to fall in love with his wife. This happens slowly at first. He begins to notice his wife's demands are different, less possessive. Then comes a freer feeling—he enjoys not looking over his shoulder, finds freedom in not worrying about what others might see. He and his wife have developed a tacit understanding of how things work; he feels a deep appreciation for their smooth and orderly life. If she has suspicions, she never voices them.

Next the sweet awakening of guilt. The urge to confess is never far from him: alongside his wife in a darkened movie theater, as he watches her work in the garden, at breakfast, sitting at their old oak kitchen table. Around him, he sees his daughters maturing. He feels his own life slipping away, as if the girls were taking his youth, inhaling it with eager, greedy breaths, trying to grow up faster. His children on the brink of becoming teens, he on the brink of what—despair? Too dramatic. Yet closer to the edge every day. And then at dinner with his family, looking into their faces, everything is clear. He has just one thought: I am a lucky man.

∿

When alone in the apartment she listens to classical music. It makes her feel as if her life has a soundtrack, like a movie. During soothing movements, she feels quieted, buffeted by the music. Louder compositions make her tense; anger and frustration swimming up close to the surface.

One late afternoon visit and the room is filled with the strains of a Strauss waltz. He pulls her close to his chest, moving perfectly in step with its one-two-three rhythm. "Don't look at your feet," he tells her. "It will only confuse you." She has heard the waltz is the closest music to a human heartbeat, music felt by the body. Pressing in close, she doesn't look down. She looks instead to her window and wonders what others peering in would see. This is not all there is, she wants to tell them. This is not the complete picture.

Then there are days she wants to tell other women in the bank line, or at the fruit stand; she wants to shout it out: I am having an affair with a married man. I have become the other woman. But when she looks around, looks at the other women standing together or alone, she remains silent, wondering if each one of them is also having a similar affair. What if the world were filled with women who shared the same experience—tight-lipped women who have to stop themselves from shouting out well-kept secrets?

And then her list of *nevers* that keeps company in her head: They will never sit down, knees touching, in front of a group of friends, and tell the story of how they met. She will never ask him: It happened this way, didn't it dear? And he will never be able to think of their being together without also thinking of what he has lost, pain he has caused.

Though just last week she awoke in full panic from a bad dream: images of a swiftly moving current, a crashing waterfall. She reached out for him, stretched her arm long toward his side of the bed, her hand open, empty. Through half-closed eyes she imagined she saw his shadowy outline: the long lines of his body, the slight protruding paunch, his face in sharp profile. She looked toward the apparition: Who are you?

And if someone were to peer into her window, would they see the woman with the imaginary lover in her bed? Would they understand as she turns, rolls over slowly, her back to him, allowing him his side of the bed, his half of the covers? A shared moment, for two, alone. Like separate coordinates—he and she—plotted on a graph: the arc of their love affair, its curve hitting the bottom of the page, reaching down to its lowest point.

Intimate Landscape

You wake up one morning and decide it's time to have a child. This is it, you tell your husband of many years. It's time. "Sex all the time?" he asks hopefully. "I'm going to enjoy this."

You announce your hopes out loud, to friends, to strangers. "Well, we're not *not* trying," you say, letting them figure it out.

For three months you try in an unscheduled, spontaneous, and hopeful lots-of-sex kind of way. "Let's make a baby," your husband says, as he leads you to the bedroom, the couch, the kitchen floor. He has the easy part.

Nothing happens.

It's time to get on the stick, you tell your husband. Literally. The sticks have arrived in your home—ones to pee on, to detect subtle midmonth shifts in your delicate hormonal balance, and then ones that announce your fate, the bright little "plus" sign, to let you know that you have successfully met your fertility objective.

Nothing happens.

You see your doctor and tell her you've been trying to get pregnant; you suspect she is relieved—her expression says, "At your age, it's about time." She tells you it takes most couples a year to get pregnant. Her advice: Relax.

You don't believe her. You have heard enough horror stories from friends your age on the fertility circuit. You book a specialist and lie through your teeth, telling them you've been trying for over a year. There will be tests. Unseemly and inconvenient and invasive tests. Submit.

You begin to live your life in twenty-eight-day cycles: fourteen days of hopefulness, then ovulation, copulation, and two more weeks of waiting until you can take the stick test. Negative results to be followed by despair and the wait for the inevitable, the walls to crumble, the feeling of a hollow vessel.

Begin again. Repeat as many times as your heart can stand it.

One day, after a year of tests that have breached your belly button, with scopes snaked through your insides, after a year of taking drugs that produce mood swings that make PMS look like a walk in the park, at a cost enough to rival the gross national product of a small country, you see a sign. That positive plus sign. Just the vaguest of blue, the faint outline of the cross, and you fall to your knees on the bathroom floor in thanks.

It's early, too early, and yet you tell everyone. Your friends begin to treat you differently, more carefully and watchfully. Your husband starts to call you "Mommy"—once, in the middle of the night, you catch him murmuring sweet nothings directly to your midsection—and you find yourself drawn to all things baby: parenting magazines, diaper commercials, children in strollers. The shift is sudden, leaving you feeling a little dizzy and off-balance. There is a new feeling of joy so overwhelming it almost hurts.

Then one afternoon when you are home on the couch, doing the crossword puzzle and drinking mineral water, the cramping starts: a low rumble between your hipbones, a burning up your legs, a tremor down your spine. It's nothing, it's nothing, it's nothing you say, willing yourself to believe.

When the cramping continues, gaining strength, you begin to pray to a force you never really believed in, the faith of strong desire, desperation, and foxholes. Your prayer takes the form of one word: Please.

Later, at the doctor's office, your husband will sit with you as blood is drawn. Together you will watch as a wand of sound displays a picture on a small screen, like the black and white television of your childhood, and there you will glimpse the peaks and valleys of an intimate landscape, empty and bare.

"Wait a few months," the doctor tells you. She squeezes your shoulder, looks into dry eyes. "There's still time," she says in her best encouraging doctor voice. "You can try again."

Try again? You don't know how you could ever try again and yet you know somehow that you will. And this feels like hope, something you never knew you had, but has been there with you all along, just lying in wait to be born.

What Remains

Ava was the type of woman who lost things easily; whole worlds slipped through her fingers at one time or another. One day it would be blue things, the mail flyer, the pen, the magazine with the dog-eared pages. Other days it would be the apartment keys, the cat's toy—that mouse with the missing eye that she called "Mr. Bumble"—her third-grade students' leaf collections, the gray-flaked snow globe bought on the New Jersey Turnpike, and once, even, the complete works of Shakespeare, the paperback copy with the tiny print, thick like a phone book. All gone.

She used to search at first, when things would go missing. A full-scale affair that would have her tearing through the apartment, looking high and low, peering under couch cushions, through desk drawers, walking in circles, her eyes wildly scanning every surface, until it all melded into one dizzy whole. Always futile. And then the hard-won acceptance. They were gone. Things might reappear, at different points in her life, days or months, or, in the case of the small heart locket given to her by her great aunt, years later. But the truth was, once she had lost something, she knew it wasn't likely to return any time soon.

~

On Tuesday night he held her tight under a lightweight blanket, his skin warm and smooth next to hers, and ran his fingers through her hair. He leaned in close, close enough to whisper in her ear: Let's never love anyone else. By Wednesday she had lost him, returned to his wife, his home, his daughter with the new hot-pink two-wheeler bike he had just taught her to ride, and a fat shedding dog named Mike.

She decided to drown her sorrows in gin and tonics and a man named Spike—a man she met halfway into her second drink at Joe's, the neighborhood bar. She liked the way Spike introduced himself, the comfortable ease as if they had been long-lost friends. His real name was Sam, he told her. He used to be an actuary in Piscataway. Insurance, he said. Boring, really.

"Assurance?" she asked.

"Insuraaance," he said again, giving the word far too many syllables. He explained to her how one day, while reading the underwriting charts for a male pencil-pusher with a desk job, he just got up and walked away. Just like that. No safe odds for him. Now he worked for his uncle. Honest labor, he said, holding up his roughed hands. There was no ring, she noticed. He wore a faded denim jacket and she liked the way he smelled like evergreens.

By her third drink, and his second—he was trying to catch up!—she started to assemble a collection of limes, lining them up along the bar, a semicircle of little green frowns, all downturned in disappointment. She told him she wasn't interested in any more relationships, that she was swearing them off for Lent. He started to call her Rebound then, instead of Ava, saying the word over and over with certain lightness in his voice.

Spike was a tile layer now.

"You know how men are like tile?" he asked her.

She looked up at him blankly.

"Lay us right once and you can walk all over us."

She remembers laughing too hard, almost choking, wiping the tears from her eyes in exaggerated movements, and then, the next morning in his apartment, she remembers how she put her entire face into a sinkful of cold water just to cool her shame.

I'm too old to be waking up in strange men's beds, she told herself, as she gathered up her clothes and tried to sneak out in semi-darkness. She was twenty-eight last summer.

I'll call you, he called out to her back before he rolled over. She never expected to hear from him again.

Spike called the next day while she was teaching and left a message. She wrote his number down on a small scrap of paper and promptly lost it. The second time he called, he left a time to meet at Joe's. No phone number. She debated with herself the whole time she was getting ready to see him—you shouldn't, she said as she pulled the black T-shirt over her head. What do I have to lose? she asked as she ran a comb through her wet hair.

A few weeks later it was Spike who carried a huge bag of potting soil up the four flights of stairs to her apartment to help her plant window boxes. It was Spike who suggested that her students, the third-graders, could build an entire city block out of milk cartons, paper towel tubes, and graph paper. He was pleased to learn how much her students loved the project. I must have been an urban planner in another life, he said.

And it was Spike's idea to take a trip to Atlantic City. Think about the beach, he said. The boardwalk, the bells ringing over the slots and the sound of all that money.

"Lost money," she said, a hollow, familiar feeling starting in her chest.

"Found money," he said. "If you're willing to risk house odds."

"The house always wins," she said. "You should know that by now."

They talked a bit on the drive, speculating if she won big she wouldn't have to work this summer, no part-time jobs when she wasn't teaching. With his winnings he would buy a motorcycle, something Italian, that was fast and sleek and reeked of high insurance premiums and danger. After all, he said, I am dating someone on the rebound; it proves I'm drawn to danger.

Their gambling money was gone more quickly than they expected and Ava found a new freedom in losing. Afterward they hit the boardwalk. She ordered a drink with an umbrella at an outdoor café and he bought colorful postcards at a gift shop. They walked together along the beach near the water and ate caramel corn from a white plastic bucket. Spike stopped once to roll up his pant leg, revealing a startling smooth white knob of an ankle that reminded her of the perfect round soaps people set out for guests, too good for daily use. She resisted the urge to lean down and touch it.

On the drive back, they didn't talk much, falling into an easy silence, free of expectations. Sunburned and tired, she rested her head against the window and closed her eyes while Spike circled looking for a parking space, finally stopping to drop her off in front of her building.

She didn't see him at first when she got out of the car, didn't see him sitting there on her stoop in his khaki pants and U. Penn sweatshirt, holding a red gym bag and looking more stray dog than returned lover. When she finally did see him, she stopped walking, unable to move. Spike got out of the car, eyed the stranger on the stoop, and tapped his keys against the roof of his red Chevy Malibu. I'll see you later, he called out, sounding more like a question than a statement. She barely turned her head in his direction to wave good-bye.

I've left my wife, were the first words he spoke as she walked toward him. He wasn't looking directly at her; instead, he peered over her shoulder to get a look at the red car and the other man. That's it, he said, turning to face her fully. I've left, I'm here to stay.

His words strung together like a rope ladder stretched out between them, a shaky, narrow bridge, slung low over a widening chasm.

How many times had she hoped to hear him say this? How many nights had she kept herself awake with thoughts of his declarations and promises, hours spent wishing for his return?

Is this all it would take, they could be a couple now—filling the days, months, and years of their lives together—if she chose to come closer?

Ava knew more about losing, the hollowness felt in the body, the emptiness of what remains. Finding was a different story. It was the other half of the picture. Love and loss entwined, a knotted tangle of grief and desire. She walked toward him then, knowing that if she didn't she would never move; she would still be there in the street, hugging her sides tightly, lost in a middle space, never finding what was within her reach.

III

STILL LIFE

I'd been trying to have an argument with my mother for days. She wanted me shipped across state lines, to a counselor-in-training program at Blue Mountain Camp for Girls; I wanted to stay home, to take a botany course in summer school. We were at an impasse, neither side budging, and when I came home from school and found her sitting on the couch, in the same place, the same exact spot I left her in that morning, I knew there was going to be trouble.

Mom was sitting quietly, flipping through a back issue of *ARTnews,* a can of Coke balanced on one knee, an ashtray on the other. Empty cigarette packs and soda cans were piled around her ankles and it looked like she was in it for the long haul, with no plans of getting up anytime soon.

I tried an imploring tactic, picking up where I'd left off that morning, when I'd slammed my way out the front. "I really need to stay and take this course."

"Why?" she asked. "Why do you *need* it?" I noticed she'd picked up my intonation. "Is that boy involved?"

She meant Josh, my lab partner, whose hands shook during frog dissection but were always so sure and steady when they held mine.

I left to heat up some Pop-Tarts. "You don't get it," I called out from the kitchen. She really didn't get it—in the past, when I'd tried to explain to her about the importance of classifying and studying plant life, she'd just looked at me blankly. My mother was not the type of person who spent too much time trying to create order in the natural world. She was just one step ahead of disorder, entropy city.

"No, you don't get it, Luce," she said quietly. Our apartment is small, and even in the kitchen, I could still hear her clearly.

My mother is a photographer, known best for her portraits of ex-wives, her only theme since my father left three years ago. In the past, there've been times when she's come home late from work, landed on the couch, and not left until after I went to bed. Refueling the jets, she called it. Decompression time. But this was different. She stayed on the couch the next day, and the day after that. I began to hesitate before turning my key in the lock, before opening the door, afraid I would see her still sitting there, her bony shoulders jutting through the same dirty green sweatshirt she was wearing on the day she took up her post.

I sat with her on the couch after school, a new routine. I rested my head in her lap and tried to think of ways I could stay and take the course. She absently stroked my hair and stared out the window. We could sit like that for hours, for as long as I could take it. I thought about friends who had to have actual conversations with their mothers and wondered if it felt strange.

If I wanted to stay in the city with Josh, I needed to get the class permission form signed by Monday. There was no way around it: If she wouldn't sign, I would have to call my father. I didn't want to get him involved. He would take the couch business as a sign that she has finally lost it—he always believed she was one step away from a breakdown, especially since the breakup, when he'd moved downtown with Bruce.

"Why is this so hard?" I said out loud.

My mother stopped stroking my hair. "Sometimes we just have to swim upstream," she said. "It's hard when you have to push against the current."

Her voice startled me. "What is that supposed to mean?" I couldn't even imagine my mother swimming; if anything, she was like one of those sea creatures, the kind that lived in their own shell, tossed along in rough current. "Do you see any water here?"

"You know what I mean," she said, picking up an empty soda can to use as an ashtray.

What I knew was that she was talking in circles, not making sense, and it made me feel like crying, not about summer school, but because it felt hard being fifteen, falling in love, and having a mother who didn't want to leave the couch.

"Why don't you tell me something helpful?" I said. "Like what you're doing here?"

"What are any of us doing here?" She folded her hands primly in her lap. She never wore gloves when she worked in the darkroom and her hands were always dried and cracked from the chemicals. People often said we looked like sisters, with our long, stick-straight brown hair, washed-out gray eyes, and those big hands. But my hands were smooth and soft, and I have never wanted to be an artist.

"Are you trying to set some kind of record?" I asked. "Is that it?"

She leaned her head back against the large green couch cushions and looked at me. "Call Guinness," she said. "This could be one for the books."

Josh's bedroom was dark green, the color of mossy riverbanks, rangy ferns, and dense underbrush, primordial and lush. He kept the shades pulled, even in the middle of the afternoon, and the only light came from four fish tanks—three freshwater, one salt—lit at the top by long silvery white tubes that shimmered and glowed, giving the whole room a dreamy underwater feeling.

We started kissing at the doorway and didn't stop, didn't break away or part until we were both lying on his bed.

"It'll be great," Josh said, slipping his arm under my head. "We're going to be able to spend the whole entire summer together." He kissed my neck and slid his hand under my T-shirt, the waistband of my jeans. "My mother doesn't get home until late these days. There will be nobody here to bother us."

Josh's mom was a lawyer at a big firm downtown with a lot of names on the door. She wore suits and serious shoes and always walked around with a travel mug of coffee, even when she wasn't going anywhere. She called me Lucille—my name is Lucinda—and had an intense way of staring at me that made feel guilty, like she was waiting for me to confess to some horrible act I'd never committed.

He ran his hand along my inner thigh. "She was actually worried I might not have enough to do this summer to keep me busy."

The bedspread felt scratchy against the back of my arms and Josh's weight pressed heavily against me, making it hard to breathe. I tried not to notice, to lose myself in his kisses, his touch. I thought about how he looked on that first day we met in biology class, his curly hair, heavy-lidded eyes, off-kilter grin, and how happy I was when we were assigned as lab partners.

When he went for the snap on my jeans, I sat up.

"I need to go home. To see my mother." I don't know why I said it; it just came out. I didn't even want to think about my mother, about how she was sitting back at the apartment, rooted on the couch. "I've got to go."

"Right now?" He pulled his hand away. "Are you kidding?" He sounded disappointed, and a little hurt.

I had a choice then: Tell him everything, or say I was joking, pull him toward me, feel his skin on mine and try to forget all about it, about her.

"She's sick," I said. "Well, not really sick, more like stuck." He looked confused and I was instantly sorry I mentioned it. I wanted to go back to where we'd just been, to feel the pressure of his hand on my body, making me feel solid again, real.

"Stuck? Like in traffic?" It was as if he were trying to figure out the next thing I was going to say before I said it. "Is she out of town?"

"No. She's in town," I said. "She's just stuck on the couch."

"Oh." He relaxed, leaned down and burrowed his face in my neck, speaking directly into my collarbone. "That happened to my dad last winter."

I felt a rush of relief. Maybe Josh could understand; maybe it wasn't as unusual as it seemed, maybe other parents went through this kind of thing, too. I pushed his shoulder back. "What happened?"

"Nothing really. Bad back. Laid him out flat for weeks. He couldn't even move, and he was totally out of it from the pain meds." Josh rolled over, stretched his legs out in front of him and looked up at the ceiling. "That stuff will mess you up."

I was disappointed. "This is different," I said. "She can get up. At least I think she can. She just doesn't want to."

Josh shifted. "She *wants* to stay on the couch?"

"Kind of," I said, feeling a little embarrassed. I wasn't sure I knew how to explain to him about a mother who sat and smoked and stared into space all day. Josh never smoked, drank, or even ate red meat—he said his body was a temple and I was quickly becoming a true believer.

"She's just taking a break from things. She's calling her time on the couch a victory for furniture. No big deal." I looked at the tank closest to me. Flat, glassy fish eyes stared back; tiny mouths opened and closed, telling me something I couldn't hear.

By Saturday morning, almost a week into my mother's couch crisis, I knew I had to call my father. I walked into the living room and announced the jig was up, that you-know-who was going to have to be brought in. "This is getting out of hand," I said in a tone I've heard parents use when they're speaking to kids behaving badly. "You've got to get off this couch. Or else."

I waited, watching to see if the mention of my father would get a reaction, if she would call my bluff.

"If he's coming over," she said, slowly holding up an empty cigarette carton, "ask him to pick up another. I'm running low."

My mother had always had her backward days; that's what my father called them. "The whole world moves through the day going forward," he'd said, "while Lily moves backward." Those were times when she would sleep through the entire day only to wake up when everybody else was going to bed. On backward days, she kept the curtains drawn and the blankets pulled tightly over her body, and it was strictly lights out and voices low around the apartment. After a day in bed she would get up in the middle of the night and start working and not stop—she might not need to sleep again for days. I grew up listening to her late-night toiling, falling asleep while she drove herself through relentless all-nighters, brimming with energy and purpose. It was as if years of restless activity were finally catching up with her. I wondered if I waited her out, let her get some rest, then, maybe, like Josh's dad, she would get up again, good as new.

When I couldn't remember the last time my mother ate anything, I went out to get pizza. She looked more tired and distant when I returned and didn't say a word when I went to my room to call my father.

I dialed and prayed Bruce wasn't home to answer. I used to have to go see my father and Bruce every other weekend, until my mother pulled the plug on the idea, saying I needed a less structured visitation schedule—in truth, she was always getting the dates mixed up, and there were often disagreements or confusion about who was supposed to "have me" for the weekend. This was fine with me, because my father was usually busy in his studio working, and that left Bruce, the eager beaver, ready to step in and try his hand at parenting, with his not-so-helpful self-improvement suggestions, like reasons I should trim my split ends, wear brighter colors, or stop biting my nails. I didn't get that kind of mothering at home; I certainly didn't want it from my father's boyfriend.

"How are things going in Botany Bay?" Bruce asked.

"Swimmingly," I said. "Is my father around?"

"I wish." He let out a long sigh. "You know your father. Try him at the studio."

I felt a little pang, and thought, for the first time, that things probably weren't so great for Bruce, either. But he was the adult; he had a choice.

Where my mother's studio was small, with plain white walls and dark floors, rectangular and even as a shoebox, my father's space was all sharp angles, alive with color and light. He was a furniture designer, and people paid a lot of money to sit in his chairs, eat at his tables, and stow their dishes in his cupboards and sideboards. "The Queen of Cabinetry," my mother called him, when she was in a sour mood.

The studio seemed empty when I walked in, though the heavy red metal door was unlocked.

"Dad?" I called out. "Anybody here?"

"Jesus!" said a voice from the back. "You scared the hell out of me." A young man walked toward me. He was wearing a bright-yellow tank top and cutoff jean shorts. When I got a better look at him, I realized he wasn't much older than me.

"I'm looking for my father," I said. "Is he around?"

"Father? You're in the wrong place, girly-girl. No daddies around here." He giggled and I noticed a flash of teeth, gleaming and straight.

"Greg Garson," I said, pointing to the furniture and artwork that lined the walls, and then to the double G logo in maroon on the front door. "Greg is my *daddy*."

"Oops," he said. "Sorry. Greg should be back any minute. I didn't know he had kids."

"Kid," I said. "Just one. And a wife. Though they're not together anymore." I don't know why I said that, why I felt it necessary to drag my mother into the conversation for the second time that day. "I'm Lucy."

"Ricky," he said, "and my parents split too, before I was born. My father took off, went back to the Dominican Republic." He said this like it was the most natural thing in the world to discuss your parents' breakup with a total stranger. He went on to tell me about how his mother worked as a live-in maid in New Jersey, and that he was raised by his grandmother in Newark.

My father showed up just as Ricky was telling me about his grandmother's amazing lacework that had people lined up at her door.

"I didn't know you were stopping by, Luce." He looked surprised and a little uneasy to see me, though he quickly tried to hide it. He introduced me to Ricky, his new studio assistant.

"I need a small favor," I said. "No big deal." I reached into my pocket for the crumpled summer school permission form. "It should only take a minute."

"Why don't we go to my office," he said, pointing to the small black door marked *Private*. "I'll be right in."

My father's desk was organized with an accuracy and precision I admired—pens soldiered neatly next to one another, papers stacked squarely, paint sample books lined up in an orderly row of straight spines. On the desk was an old photo of him, one my mother had taken when she was pregnant with me. There was a story that went with the photo, the one family story my father loved to tell, about how he came home one day to find her standing in the bathroom—her old darkroom—completely naked, sliding that picture across her swollen stomach. The part that gets to him though, the part that always makes him lower his voice and sound choked up, is what my mother was saying when he walked in, how he found her whispering, "This is your father," over and over. As God is his witness, he always says, he will never forget that sight.

I always hated that story and couldn't stand to look at that photo—his hair thick and long over his ears and collar, his eyes smiling, young—because I knew how she got when she worked. I could easily picture her standing there, her long hair piled on top of her head, held in place with a pencil or clothespin, the stray uneven pieces that always came undone getting tucked back again and again behind her ear. She was totally naked because she couldn't stand the feel of clothes against her tightly stretched skin. I could see her taking the photo, placing it face-down against her skin, circumnavigating it around the stark white globe of her belly. There would be that look on her face, one I have seen too many times, of being there and not being there. And me, swimming around tadpole-style, submerged, sensing the ripples on the surface, feeling the gentle pressure and hearing the word "father" for the first time.

"Botany class," I said to my father when he came in the room. "Summer school permission form, something I really want to take and that looks good on the college transcript."

"I thought we settled on camp for you. I signed those forms a month ago." He sat down at his desk. "That's so like your mother to change her mind at the last minute—is she okay?"

"Hanging in there," I lied. "Nothing to report."

"She didn't sound too good last time we spoke. She kept going on about how you're going to go away to camp. She wouldn't let it drop. She was pretty worked up about it. And now she's changed her mind?"

"Yeah," I said. "You never can tell with her." I felt the cold sting of my betrayal. "Besides, I never wanted to go to camp. I wanted to stay here, to take a summer school class."

He leaned back in his chair. "And your mother agreed?"

"Sort of. She's been kind of preoccupied lately. I thought you could sign for her."

I was caught and I could tell he knew it.

"Camp's not that bad, you know. It could be a lot of fun."

"Macaroni art," I said. "Lanyard key rings. Pinecone ashtrays." I was grasping at anything, hoping bad art would be his breaking point.

"And that counselor-in-training stuff looks good on the applications—it shows you can handle responsibility."

"Responsibility?" It felt hopeless—everyone wanted me to go away. "I handle *my* responsibilities just fine."

"Give it a rest." He sat back in his chair and went on about the beauty of the outdoors, the woods and streams he remembered from his childhood summer trips to the country.

"Your mother also seemed concerned about this boyfriend you've been spending a lot of time with lately."

So she wanted to ship me off to camp to keep me away from Josh? It made no sense. I felt angry and I hated them both in that moment.

"That's funny. When I spoke to Bruce today, he seemed a little concerned about how much time you're spending here with your new boyfriend." I nodded toward the door, toward the studio where I'd met Ricky. It felt good to say it, in a powerful and scary way.

I expected him to be furious, but he just laughed and shook his head. "It might do you some good to go away. You seem to have gotten a little cynical and hard-edged lately."

He sounded so sure of himself, so knowing. "Your mother might be on to something."

"The only thing my mother is on to is the couch," I said. "She hasn't left it in almost a week." It was a relief to say it out loud.

He sat up straight in his seat, his smile gone. "What do you mean? What happened?"

"Don't worry," I said. "She's not your wife anymore, not your *responsibility*." She really wasn't his responsibility, though I wasn't sure when she had become mine.

I watched as he ran his hand through his thinning hair. "Why didn't you call me?" His voice was sharp. He stood up from behind the desk like he was going to reach across and grab me.

"Why should I call you?"

"It sounds like your mother's in trouble."

I felt a thin pang of shame for not telling him sooner. "There's nothing you can do about it. She's just taking some time off from life."

"We'll see about that," he said, picking up the phone. I listened as he canceled dinner plans with Bruce and said he had to see my mother, that she was really losing it this time.

Back in the apartment, I settled in next to Mom on the couch, careful not to upset her precarious balancing act of ashtray and soda can. The gray tips of the river were barely visible from the window, and I wondered if this was what she'd been staring at all day, the water.

"I saw Dad," I said.

She barely nodded in response, her chin slowly moving toward her chest.

"He thinks the botany course sounds like a natural fit, that I'm probably not cut out for the whole counselor thing, anyhow."

My mother inhaled, taking a long, deep drag from her cigarette. I waited for her to say something, anything.

"He's going to stop by soon," I said.

She pulled at the hem of her sweatshirt and stretched it out close to her knees. Long after being in the darkroom, hands scrubbed raw, my mother always smelled like her work, a combination of Dektol and fixer permeating her skin. As I sat next to her in the fading light, it was that smell, or lack of smell, that finally got to me. I always assumed it would be there, part of her, like the mole below her left eye, or the wedding ring she never took off. Its absence filled me with sadness; it reminded me of things I had lost, and made me long for those nights when she would come home, energized after work, and stand at the sink drinking glass after glass of water, trying to flush the chemicals out of her system. Without gloves the chemicals got in her blood, giving her a cold metallic chill that ran through her, filling her mouth with a taste she described as sweet and sad at the same time. I used to argue that sad wasn't something you could taste, but she always insisted it was, a taste she hoped I would never acquire.

I left her and called Hunan Palace, adding steamed dumplings and another egg roll to our usual order. At the sink, packed with dirty dishes and fast food containers, I scraped and washed off some plates, even though I knew my mother, if she ate at all, would easily prefer the steaming white takeout box. Behind me, our refrigerator held only film canisters, cans of soda, and the light. I set the coffee table for dinner, aligning the plates carefully, and pulled over one of Dad's hand-painted canvas chairs.

Our dining table was buried under a broken enlarger, stacks of negatives encased in plastic sheeting, and a thick layer of dust. I ran my fingers across it, traced my initials on its surface. When my father lived here, he cleaned—he was the one who washed dinner dishes, made beds, straightened counters, scoured the tub, ran a damp mop across the hardwoods. If he were still here, the table would have shone, polished to a high gloss. Now it sat in the corner, coated in an ash-gray dust thick enough to sift. If I went back through the layers I could probably find dust from the night he left; that gray November day, three years ago, when we drove upstate for a hike, though that was the excuse, so he could tell me he was leaving. Life with your mother is too hard, is what he said, he couldn't live with us anymore. We walked together in silence under bare limbs, along a dried veil of leaves. When he dropped me off later, he said it was better if he didn't come up, that his bags were already packed in the trunk. I stood on the sidewalk that night and watched as he pulled away from the curb.

The buzzer rang. He walked in bearing dinner and that old forced smile, the one I remembered from when he still lived here—lips tight and scrunched up in the corners. I could tell he was surprised by the mess, the way he looked around and took it all in. Scanning two rooms at a time.

"Ran into the delivery guy downstairs," he said, handing me the food bag and making a beeline for the couch, sitting down close beside Mom.

"Greg?" she said. Her eyes drooped heavily and it seemed like she carried years of tiredness in her body. She kind of wilted onto his shoulder, folding herself into him like she was going to take a nap.

He pushed her straight hair away from her face and rested his chin on the top of her head. He spoke to her like he would speak to a child, repeated words and sounds—"Shh" and "It's okay"—over and over in small whispers.

"I'm so tired," she said. He absently patted the seat next to him for me to join them, but I pretended not to see, busy fixing her plate, making sure the different foods didn't touch.

He wrapped his arms tightly around her shoulder, propping her up against him. "Everything is going to be alright now."

She barely opened her eyes to look at the plate I set down in front of her. Dad talked calmly about leaving the city— over the bridge, up the thruway, to somewhere quiet, upstate, a place where an old friend, some printmaker, once went. "It's nice up there Lil, very restful." He was doing a better selling job than he did with camp and I started to get nervous, a cold line of sweat running down my spine.

I reached across and touched her arm. "Mom? Are you listening? We don't need this. You don't need to go away." I wanted to make her see what was about to happen, how she was about to lose her place on the couch permanently if she didn't snap out of it.

"Lucinda," he said. "Settle down." He used his grown-up voice with me, the one he uses on the phone when he's talking to important clients, the one that says he's in charge.

"She's not going," I said.

"Your mother needs help."

"She's fine," I said, even as my mother's head was hanging limply to one side. "No thanks to you."

"Fine? Take a look at this place." He motioned toward my mother's piles, the ashtrays overflowing with stubbed-out cigarettes, the empty cartons, discarded cans and crusty plates. "You're not fine. She's not fine. Nobody here is fine."

He turned his head toward her ear and continued to unweave our lives, talking in a low, crooning voice about how I would stay in the city with him and take the botany course—that Mom was the one who should go away for a while.

If my mother went away I could stay—even if it meant living with Dad and Bruce—and be with Josh; just the thought of it gave me a jolt, an excited thrill in my stomach. It was everything I wanted. I looked over at my mother: Her greasy hair was plastered flat against her head; she was pale and thin, the ridge of shoulder bone now poking through her sweatshirt. My heart sank. I realized she probably saw this coming, like a change in barometric pressure, a black mist moving in. She wanted me away at camp so she could enjoy her breakdown in peace, with nobody here to stare at her, to expect anything from her, to want her to get better.

"I'll go to camp," I said slowly. "She just needs some rest without me around."

"This isn't about camp anymore," he said. "Can't you see she's not getting better?"

I took my mother's arm. "You can't take her away," I said, and tried to pull her away from him, pushing hard against the current.

"Stop it," he said, raising his voice. "You're acting as crazy as she is."

I pulled my mother again and he actually grabbed her other arm and pulled back, hard enough to make me worry she would split in two, right down the middle, like a rag doll. "Let go," he said.

I wanted to put my hands over my ears, close my eyes tightly, to chant or hum the way I did when I was small and didn't want to hear something disturbing. But instead I kept pulling, tugging on her, trying to move her toward the door.

"Stop it," he said again. He was standing now, holding onto my mother's shoulders, trying to keep her in place.

I was crying. My mother's eyes were open and dazed, vacant as a sleepwalker, or a zombie in a cheesy horror movie.

"She's not going," I said. "Why does everybody around here always have to leave?" I pulled her again, as hard as I could. My father let go this time, and my mother slid from the couch and fell on top of me, pushing me backward to the floor.

Her weight pressed full against me, covering me completely, pinning me to the ground. He rushed over, trying to undo the tangle of arms and legs. I felt him take her from me, lifting her easily, like she weighed nothing, an empty shell. He sat down on the floor next to me, my mother on her side, knees curled to her chest; he fastened his arms around my shoulders and tried to rock me back and forth like a baby.

I wriggled away as he talked in a quiet voice about how things were going to get better, that we would all be alright. I wasn't really listening. I was holding my breath as if underwater, watching how the moonlight through our window burned away the shadows. I knew she would have seen this, sitting here night after night, submerged as the growing light rippled across the floor. He said my name, trying to call me back. I thought about her stillness, her vision compressed to a single frame. He reached out his arm to hold me, finally resting his hand between my shoulder and neck. There are bulbs that look similar before they're planted, I wanted to tell him, but are nothing alike after they've bloomed. He was shaking his head, like he was trying to make sense of what had just happened. I wanted to explain how a frail flower, reedy asparagus, and wild onion could all be part of the same family. *Liliaceae.* The lily family. My mother let out a small moan and he turned to her, called away before I could tell him that although these differ, their thin stalks always lean, stretch out, and reach toward the light.

VISITATION RIGHTS

My mother is psychic. She has second sight. "A family gift," she says often. "Or a curse, depending on how you look at it." My grandmother also has the gift. All the women on the Ryan side of the family have it; a female legacy passed down mother to daughter through the generations, a common trait like strong nails or curly hair. Until me.

"I just don't understand it," my grandmother says, shaking her head sadly. "It makes no sense; I can see it right here." She pushes her glasses up to the top of her forehead, squints her eyes and looks again at my palm. "You have the gift as plain as day. See for yourself."

She holds my own hand up to me to examine, as if I could see it by simply looking. We are sitting outside on my grandmother's stoop in Brooklyn, a warm, windy day in March. I am nine years old. My mother is sitting next to me, humming a song about the breeze and the trees and I am staring at my own hand, looking for clues in the crooked-looking M that marks the center of my palm.

"Where does it say that?" I ask, staring at my empty hand.

My mother laughs. "You're barking up the wrong tree with Missy," she says, taking my hands in hers. "Don't even bother.

She doesn't know how to open her eyes; she has to think about everything too much."

"It's right there," says my grandmother, taking my hand back and showing it to my mother. "Plain as the nose on your face."

"Maybe," says my mother. "But I wouldn't count on it."

My mother doesn't believe in anything she hasn't seen herself, firsthand. And she's seen a lot. She has visions. Usually they happen around dinnertime, after her second scotch and soda, minus the soda. She can see around corners, knows who is about to ring the doorbell, what grades I get in school, when the phone will ring. But those are minor things. Her big showstopper is that she can communicate with the dead. She has the ability to deliver messages from the other side, a talent always strongest in November. "It's the weather," she always says, pulling her sweater in close around her. "Less interference this time of year."

For some reason dinner is the perfect time for otherworld guests to drop by. It is not unusual for my mother to look up from a steaming plate of food and announce that a recently deceased friend, neighbor, or relative is with us. "Mrs. Abrams is now in the room," my mother says in a welcoming voice, putting down her soup spoon and smiling. Pearl Abrams was the previous owner of our house; she died the summer after we moved in. "She wants to see what we've done with the place."

"How does she look?" my father asks, not looking up from his plate.

"Not bad," my mother says. "More tan than I remember, like she just came back from Miami Beach."

Novembers are always a busy time for spirit traffic around the house. Once, in the middle of the night, all the dogs in the neighborhood started howling, keening the same low moan. The sound woke me up and sent me running to my parents' room, terrified that something was horribly wrong.

"Shh. Don't be scared," my mother said, lifting the blankets and moving over to make room for me in the bed. I settled down into the warm spot where her body had just been. "It's Harry Stevens from across the street," she said, mentioning the neighbor boy who had drowned while away at summer camp. "He wants his mother to know he's alright, that he's just late getting home." I fell back to sleep that night snuggled in close, curled up under her arm, a baby chick under the wing, while she continued her conversation in low murmured tones with a boy I couldn't see.

My grandmother draws the line at nocturnal visits from the other world. "If you can't stop by at a decent hour, don't bother," she says. "I can't be up all night communing with the spirits. I need my beauty rest."

My grandmother really is a beauty. She's drawn appreciative stares and comments all her life from both men and women for her black curly hair, piercing blue eyes, and what she calls her "dancer's legs." No one has ever seen her in long pants.

Things between my grandmother and mother never go smoothly. Their connection is strong and volatile, filled with high drama and hurt feelings; I guess it's easy for their feelings to get hurt when they can read each other's minds. During their many arguments it's not unusual for my mother to point at the phone, seconds before it rings, and say, "That's your grandmother; tell her I'm not here." My grandmother does the same, waving a finger toward the old black wall phone and announcing, "Your mother is about to call; please ignore it."

When my mother and grandmother are on speaking terms, all is right with the world. My grandmother calls for long phone chats and my mother always lets me speak to her first. I hold the receiver close to my ear and listen to my grandmother's soft voice and the gentle *swoosh, swoosh* of tarot cards in the background. Those cards are her constant companion and she keeps them either in her hands or wrapped in a square piece of linen tucked tightly under her pillow while she sleeps. Cards, tea leaves, palms: My grandmother reads them all; everything is a sign, warning, a prediction or portent.

It rained the day my mother married my father, on a day that called for sunshine and blue skies. "God's tears," my grandmother said, her disapproval of my mother's marriage no secret. "It's a sign," she said. "This should not happen."

My grandmother has never approved of my mother's marriage—my father is twenty-five years older than my mother and working on his third marriage, not exactly what my grandmother had in mind for her only daughter. She and my mother didn't speak for thirteen months after my parents were married, until I was born. When my grandmother came to the hospital to see the baby and to collect the placenta to bury it in the backyard, my mother held me out to her as a peace offering: a chance to do things right with this daughter.

"We'll call her Melissa," my grandmother said. My mother agreed, shortening the name quickly to "Missy."

My grandmother takes an active hand in my raising and I spend weekends, holidays, entire summers in the same brownstone where my mother was raised, sleeping in her childhood bed, playing with what is left of her toys. I am entirely devoted to my grandmother, her constancy and unconditional love, but when it comes to training me to read cards, to see the next foot about to fall, I am hopeless. "You'll get it one day," my grandmother always promises. "Don't feel bad. You're just a late bloomer."

If ghostly visitors aren't enough, November is also the time of year when strange things happen at my house. We never know why the dryer suddenly starts in the middle of the night, making a *thump-thump* sound like it's filled with tennis sneakers, or why things carefully placed in one spot at night—keys, books, briefcase—disappear in the morning, only to reappear somewhere else days later. And why once, for an entire week after dinner, all the lights in the house began to blink on and off in a steady three-second, two-second pattern, as even as labor pains.

"Blame the Haller," my mother says, not concerned by the strange occurrences. Growing up, I assume every house has a Haller, a playful spirit, common as a house cat, that pulls off mischievous pranks. Like the tooth fairy, the Haller is part of my childhood, something I don't quite believe in, yet am always surprised by when it shows up.

No matter what the Haller does, or who shows up floating unexpectedly over our dinner table, nothing can diminish my excitement about Guy Fawkes Day. It's the one holiday my parents really get behind and celebrate, the one holiday they both feel makes sense—other holidays are considered either too commercial or made up by the greeting card companies. "Just an excuse to make money," my father says. He is an atheist who believes in no greater power than himself. My mother, who claims to like the feeling of church, though she has never attended, wakes up every morning and says out loud: "This is the day the Lord hath made, let me rejoice therein." But that's where it stops; all other worship is done of each other. What my parents have lost in organized religion, they have made up in their faith in finding one another.

Over the years my parents' Guy Fawkes party has become legendary; it starts after sundown and continues into the early morning hours, ending with burning a fully clothed scarecrow—a likeness of Guy Fawkes, a person who actually tried to blow up the British Parliament—in a large bonfire in the backyard.

By late October my grandmother begins her lobbying for me to spend Guy Fawkes with her, arguing that I don't need to be around such drunken revelry. "Our ancestors were burned at the stake," she says. "Why do you want to glorify this type of

Visitation Rights

behavior?" Some years she wins; other years my mother wins, depending on which way the wind blows.

The November I turn twelve, my mother's ex-boyfriend Willy starts visiting. On long, cold evenings when my father is out at a committee or local council meeting, Willy stops by. He was a pharmacist, shot dead in the street in Sheepshead Bay on his way to visit my mother. Now he has finally found his way back to her. On these nights, the house fills with the strong smell of pipe smoke and bourbon, a strange combination, so strong that even I, who usually see nothing, can't deny it. "What is that?" I ask my mother. "Go to your room," she says. "I have some unfinished business here."

Willy's visits leave my mother weepy, have her refreshing her drink several times and singing "It Had to Be You" in a throaty, off-kilter voice. I lie on my bedroom floor next to the heat register, listening to her sing and waiting for my father to come home. When he does, his voice mixes with my mother's and rises with the warm air to the second story of our house, finding its way through the register to my ear. Each snippet of conversation comes with a warm blast of air, calming me until I feel sleepy and reassured that everything will be alright.

The year I turn twelve, my grandmother wins the Guy Fawkes discussion without an argument. "I need some time to rest," my mother tells me as I am shipped off with an overnight bag and the promise of a quick return, though it will actually be two weeks before my parents will get around to picking me up again.

131

"It's time," my grandmother says. "You're almost grown up, a woman. We need to have an important talk about how things work in this world; you should know some things."

We are sitting in her yellow kitchen at a Formica-topped table flecked with gold stars.

"If this is about getting my period, we've already had that talk in school," I tell her, trying to act bored by the whole topic.

"Please," she says. "This is about energy. People give off a color or a feeling. It's time for you to learn these things. Has your mother taught you nothing? Look at me, look hard and you will be able to see it."

I look for what feels like hours, trying, sitting and squinting my eyes, staring at her until my vision becomes blurry and doubled. Nothing.

"Relax," she says. "You're looking the wrong way. Try it again, only this time close your eyes."

My parents call two days after the party. My grandmother sends me out of the room before the phone rings, even though I can hear her clearly through the wall, warning my mother about the dangers of missed school and truancy. I don't have to be psychic to hear my mother's full-throated laugh, her voice when she says to her mother, "Missy has enough to learn from you; don't worry about a few missed school days."

"Don't worry about your parents," my grandmother says when she hangs up the phone. "Unfortunately, they will be just fine."

I find this reassuring and watch as my grandmother lays her cards out in a simple cross on the table. I am not allowed to touch her deck. The cards are worn thin and, in places, the light actually shows through. For the first time, I am given my own deck, a bright yellow box with a magician on the cover. I am told to copy her pattern with stiff cards that do not bend easily in an unpracticed hand. I am twelve years old, I miss my parents, and this is a game that doesn't interest me.

"Look at the pictures," my grandmother tells me. "Don't worry about the words, or what they are supposed to mean; just look and tell me what you see."

I look closely at the patterns, the colors of hair and images of water; women in gowns, the men in armor.

"Look at the wands," my grandmother says, pronouncing it as *wants*. "The coins, the cups."

"I don't know what I see," I say. "It just looks like a bunch of stupid pictures. They don't make any sense to me. Let me try your deck."

My grandmother is reluctant to part with her cards. "Here, I will lay them out for you. Look at them and just tell me a story, say something, anything. It doesn't have to be true."

"What kind of story isn't true?" I ask.

"Some of the best ones," she says.

I look at the cards again. There is something in knowing I can make up anything I want that feels good, a freedom to lie. I point to a woman kneeling by the water and begin to tell a story about a curly-haired woman with light eyes who spends her summers by the water. I point to another card, describe a black-haired man, a photographer, who likes to take the woman's picture. Suddenly, I can see the scene. This is a sad story, I say. The couple can never be together; he is older, married, and Catholic, with several children and a sick mother who lives with them. I close my eyes and see the man as he teaches the young woman to drive an old blue pickup truck. He has patient eyes that crinkle in the corner when he smiles, a gap between his front teeth, and large hands that grip the wheel with ease.

I am enjoying telling this story. My eyes are closed and I can see it all. "There's a secret here," I tell my grandmother. "An important part that nobody ever knew."

"What?" she asks. "What is it?"

"Years later," I say, "before he died, he tried to find the woman again."

"Really?" my grandmother asks. She sounds surprised for the first time ever.

"Yes," I say. "He couldn't find her. But even on his deathbed he called out for her; he didn't care who heard him. He swore with his last breath that she was his one true love."

My grandmother pushes herself away from the table. I open my eyes. The moment passes. "That's enough for today," she says, dabbing at the corners of her eyes with a tissue as she leaves the room. She will never ask me to read her cards again.

As word of my mother's abilities spreads in our small town, she is called in for police work, even taking part in interrogations, considered an expert in decoding the nuances of a small gesture, reading the truth in faces and alibis. A local celebrity. My grandmother is mortified and tells her not to call attention to herself. "The villagers will turn on you," she warns. "Be careful."

In high school my friends actually think my mother's notoriety is cool, making me almost cool by association. Friends want to know if I can read their palms, if I can tell them when they're going to meet their true loves, if they're ever going to marry.

My newfound low-level popularity keeps me busy with parties, late-night phone calls, and boys. I don't have time to travel to Brooklyn, to see my grandmother, to have her instruct me on the fine interpretation of auras and card reading. And part of me is relieved.

My best friend, Elizabeth, believes in astral projection; she is drawn to the idea of floating above her own body, flying around the room tethered to her sleeping self by only a spidery silver cord. Elizabeth reads everything she can on this, buys magazines, listens to suggestive tapes on headphones at night before falling asleep. She fills my head with stories, like the one of the boy who wakes up after soaring through the sky only to have feathers fall from his bed in the morning. She believes it is only a matter of practice, that one day she will fly and when she does, she has only one destination: my mother's bedroom.

"Your mother will be the one to see me," she says. "She will prove that it works, that it's not just a dream."

Frankly, I want no part in Elizabeth's obsession. "We're not meant to go flying around without our bodies in the middle of the night," I tell her. "That is just plain crazy."

One morning my mother comes to breakfast late, an annoyed look on her face. She points to the phone and says, "Tell your friend to go bother her own mother. Leave me out of it; I didn't get any sleep last night." The phone rings. It's Elizabeth, telling me of her strange dream of flying, of seeing my mother holding lights in each hand, waving her on like an air traffic controller, and the sign she wore around her neck that said: "Stay home!"

My grandmother gets sick when I turn seventeen. I cut school, take a bus and then a subway just to see her. I do this every Wednesday for a month until I am caught, the school calling to inquire about my unusual absence pattern. My mother isn't upset by the news, not surprised to hear of my weekly visits. "The authorities are on to you," she jokes. "Time to lay low, if you ever want to graduate."

My grandmother is never surprised to see me standing on her doorstep, as if me showing up sixty miles from home is an everyday occurrence. She rushes me in, all flurry and excitement, as if she doesn't want the neighbors to see.

"We don't have much time," she says. "I have so much to tell you."

Her skin is pale and translucent, a blue-veined roadmap running beneath the surface. Her blonde pageboy wig sits sideways on her head, put on quickly for my benefit.

"Blonde?" I ask, surprised at the change from her normal dark, curly hair.

"They have more fun," she says. "So far, it's not true." She tries to straighten her hair for a minute and then gives up. "Listen," she says. "I'm not going to be around much longer, and we've got a lot of ground to cover before I go."

I don't want to hear this, don't believe there can ever be a world without her in it. "Don't be dramatic," I say. "You're doing really well."

"I'll be dead in a year," she says.

I watch as she lights a cigarette, her hands shaky.

"I want to tell you a few things before it's too late," she says. "Before they have so many damn tubes and drugs in me that I can't think straight."

"Some people would say you never thought straight to begin with," I say, hoping to change the topic.

"Well, it's better to think in circles, if you ask me," she says. "I was hoping you'd come today. I wanted to tell you something important, something you should know that might make you feel better: I am going to come back and I am going to visit you."

"Oh no, that's not my department," I say. "Talk to Mom."

"Even if I were speaking to your mother right now, which I am not, I am talking to you. This is absolutely your department, always has been. It runs stronger in you than in any of us; even your own father can see that."

There has never been any love lost between my grand-mother and father; they can barely be in the same room together, and I am surprised to hear her say anything remotely nice about him.

"He never objected to it," she continues. "Sure, we've all seen him roll his eyes, call it the Ryan mumbo jumbo, but he's never stopped it. This is my fault now. I could never depend on your mother to teach you properly. I thought I would do it, that I could do it better, and now look at me; I'm not much use to anybody."

"You're of use to me," I say, reaching for her hand. "I need you."

"Don't worry," she says, "it's not over. I am coming back. Like Houdini; you know how he always said he would come back on Halloween? Well, me too."

"What do you mean, 'me too'?"

"I mean, it seems like a good day," she says. "Good enough for him, good enough for me. I've decided to come back then. I will see you again next Halloween."

"Don't you dare," I say. "That's the last thing I need, you floating around my bed freaking me out. Don't do it. Call on Mom. She gets better reception; her satellites can pick you up from miles away."

"What is this?" My grandmother looks hurt. "Don't you want to see me again? I can't believe you would turn down the request of a dying woman."

"Sure," I say. "Come on over. Why don't you bring Stella from your old canasta group? We'll have a party."

I turn eighteen, my grandmother dies, and I move out of my home for good. I live in urban student housing, with cement-block walls, in one room with one window. In this home, everything is orderly. When you put something down in the evening, it is in the same place in the morning; there is no house spirit here to play tricks. It is heaven.

My mother drops by the week before Halloween and leaves a bottle of Johnnie Walker Black as an apartment-warming gift—"So you'll have something to offer me when I come to visit."

Before she leaves, she asks about my grandmother, about her dying wishes. The two were never able to reconcile, fighting even on my grandmother's deathbed, arguing about funeral arrangements and the guest list and menu for the wake.

"Did she ever say anything to you? Did she mention anything about returning for a visit?" She asks this casually, as if my grandmother is merely around the corner, someplace close enough where she can stop in and say hello.

"Yeah, a long time ago," I say. "She talked about seeing me on Halloween."

"Only you?" my mother asks, her nose already out of joint, as if my grandmother and I are cutting her out of our little afterworld reunion party.

"As far as I know; it sounded like I was the only person on her travel itinerary."

"I wouldn't joke if I were you," my mother says. "And if that's the case, I would clean up a little bit before she gets here." My mother looks around my tiny room. "She was always such a pain in the ass about clutter."

The first Halloween in my apartment and I choose to be alone. If my grandmother is coming, I don't want anyone or anything to scare her off.

I sit and wait, not sure what I should be doing. I clean up a bit, flip through magazines, make sure the phone is working, as if she might call to tell me she's running late, that I shouldn't worry. In all the years my mother has seen spirits floating over our dining room table, I've never asked her how it's done, what to expect, what to do.

I take out a jelly glass, one from my grandmother's own house, and open my mother's bottle of Johnnie Walker. The one thing I do know: My mother never saw anybody when she was sober.

The phone rings and I feel like I'm going to jump out of my skin. My boyfriend asks how I am doing.

"How am I doing? I am sitting here drinking alone on Halloween, waiting for a spirit that I won't be able to see. I have become a cliché. Or worse yet, my mother."

He tells me to get some rest. If she's coming, she's sure to wake me up. Spirit visits are probably not something easily slept through.

The second glass goes down easier than the first. I can barely feel my jaw at this point and my head feels light, like it could float away, and I swear if the tiny hotplate on the counter had an aura it would be purple. I can see it clearly. Definitely purple. I vow to look up what purple means in the world of auras and appliances in the morning and wonder if it is some kind of cosmic comment on my cooking.

At ten thirty I can barely keep my eyes open. "This is stupid," I say out loud. "Stupid, stupid, stupid." I pour a third glass and feel that lifting feeling, as if I am ready for takeoff. The thought of flying around the room makes me laugh and feel dizzy at the same time, my world tilting slightly to the left. I feel hopelessly tired, the force of gravity on my skin pulling me toward the bed.

The phone rings loudly enough to rattle my eyeballs in their sockets. My mother, cheery and excited, on the other end: "So, did you see her?" she asks. "How was the visit?"

My head aches, my neck is stiff, and I can barely hold the phone to my ear. "No," I say, my tongue thick and heavy. I notice the third glass of scotch is still full and sitting on the nightstand with a pair of my white lace panties underneath as a coaster.

"What is wrong with you?" my mother asks. "Are you hung over?" She says this with an incredulous tone, the voice of a person who can drink all night long and never feel bad in the morning. I nod my head, cradling the receiver to my shoulder.

"Oh honey, why? Why did you do that?"

My head throbs and I feel sick. I have a lump in my throat, like I could either cry or throw up. I feel like a kid who slept through Christmas, who missed all the big excitement and will never get it back. "I wanted to see her," I said, fighting back tears. "I thought it would help."

"All you had to do was look," she says, quietly. "There's no big magic trick here."

"Did you see her?" I ask. "Did she at least contact *you*?"

"No," my mother says, sadly. "I think she's still angry at me about inviting Uncle Andy to the funeral service. She clearly didn't want to see me again." It was my mother's turn to sound like she was going to cry. I could hear the hurt in her voice.

"Why would she pick me?" I ask. "She knew I was never any good at this stuff; I told her that you were the one she should see, not me."

"You told her that?" my mother asked. "When did you tell her that? What did she say?"

And then I have a sinking feeling, a vision, like seeing your own face in the mirror clearly for the first time. "Did you know I would drink too much last night?" I ask.

"What do you mean?" she asks.

"Did you leave that bottle, knowing I would drink it, because you were angry at me—angry that she chose to visit me?"

"That is crazy," my mother says. "Don't blame me if you're upset this morning because you had a few drinks too many last night. That is clearly not my fault."

"You knew," I say. "You knew all along that I would be nervous. You set me up and now I missed the one chance I had to see her again, my one opportunity. How could you do that to me?"

"Oh, there will be other times," my mother says. "There's always next year."

I hang up on my mother before she says good-bye. And I know, before the phone rings a few seconds later, that it's her calling back, to talk her way out of it. I already know what she's going to say—that I am being ridiculous, that I am wrong, that I am not thinking clearly—I can hear it all without picking up the receiver. The phone continues ringing. And when it finally stops I know my mother has fully heard the sound of my rejection.

I sit up. The bed spins and my stomach does a little flip. I look down and for the first time I realize I am wearing a white nightgown with small pink flowers, one I barely remember taking with me when I left home. It's an old-fashioned flannel number, with a high neck and long sleeves, and it reaches almost down to my ankles. A strange unwanted gift I have never worn, stuck in the back of the closet, one that I have called my "granny nightie".

It feels hard to move and I realize I am tucked in bed tightly, under a top sheet and blanket, both folded neatly into the mattress, with hospital corners. The room feels cool to me, and I notice that my one window, painted shut since I moved in, is now open, a breeze blowing the metal blinds against the window.

I don't remember getting ready for bed, though the practical side of me is sure I must have done this, must have dressed myself in this silly nightgown, pried open the painted window with drunken-powered strength, and then tucked myself in somehow, in a way I never have—I always kick away my blankets, earning the nickname "The Human Cyclone" because I can't stand the feeling of having anything pinning down my arms or legs.

And then, I have a clear memory. I can't be more than six years old, being put to bed, not by my mother, who would never care about things like proper sleepwear or top sheets, but by my grandmother. I am in bed and watch as her hands fold the sheets underneath the mattress. I listen to the reassuring sound of her brisk movements as she works the bedding, pulling the blankets in tight and firm. After I am tucked in she sits quietly with me, by my side steady and true, coming close only once to brush my bangs away from my forehead and graze my brow with her warm, dry lips. Secure, I know she will stay there, in the dark, waiting with me till I fall asleep.

As I close my eyes and drift off, I feel myself dipping into the strong current of memory: I can hear her clearly now, in that small, faint whisper, as she says "Goodnight." I know now that she has been here, called up whole from memory, certain as only a child can be who has seen, at the end of the day, the unsteady world put right.

LOCAL GIRL

I was sixteen the summer I met Gary Singer. He was thirty-six, and the first thing he called me was jailbait. Gary was a playwright, his wife, Sherry, an actress, and I was the babysitter; my responsibilities included walking their two daughters, Emma and Jane, to Sunny Day camp, picking them up after, playing with them at the lake, cooking dinner—mac-n-cheese, straight from the box—and putting them to bed. Easy stuff, for which I was paid three dollars an hour.

The Singers owned a small blue bungalow at the end of a long gravel driveway on Rosemary Lane, not far from my parents' home. They were summer people, tourists who followed the Hudson River away from Manhattan toward greener pastures as soon as the weather turned hot and the schools let out. If you looked at the map, ran your finger along the river for about 60 miles or so north of the city, it would lead you straight to our town, a summer haven for people escaping their city lives and city selves; a sleepy place with lakes, farms, and mom-and-pop stores at the foothills of the Catskill Mountains.

The Singer house was a small three-bedroom affair, with an A-frame shed in the backyard where Gary wrote. Inside the house, the furniture was slip-covered couches and chairs with throw pillows and loose woven rugs. Every window had gauzy white curtains and there was a rickety old card table in the kitchen. The wood-paneled walls were decorated with posters from Gary's plays, a set of matching farm landscapes painted by a friend, and several black-and-white photos of the girls and Sherry, instantly recognizable to me from the hours I spent in front of the television—she was the commercial mom, the one who couldn't get those stubborn stains out of Tommy's jeans, the one who liked to admire her reflection in her no-wax kitchen floors and who loved to make delicious-tasting cakes from a box.

Sherry spent most of that summer in L.A. shooting a pilot and going on auditions, while Gary worked fourteen hours a day in the little house out back. "Deadlines keep the heart pumping," he would announce, thumping his chest with his fist on his way through the house for something to eat or drink. "Panic is a good thing. It reminds us we're alive."

The Singers always said "cottage," never "bungalow," and that first summer they dubbed the house "Idylwylde," a name they hung on a big wooden plaque over the front door. Gary also referred to it as "the house that TV bought," which they did not put on a plaque. I always thought the second name was funny, because they didn't even own a television set.

What the Singers did own were books; they were everywhere, lining the walls, spilling from shelves, pooling around the couch legs and weighing down just about any available surface—tables, countertops, chairs. And these were only their summer books. "You should see our place in the city," Gary said. "The public library could open an annex." This was only their part-time home, everything here a copy or second-best, the good stuff saved for their real life. A whole new world to me, two houses for one family; where I lived, two miles down the same road, we had six people and one bathroom.

I met the girls first. Emma and Jane were playing outside in the yard and ran straight to the edge of the driveway when they saw me, thrilled to have someone new to talk to. When I asked if they needed a babysitter they practically dragged me to meet their father. "Do we ever," said Emma, the eight-year-old, rolling her eyes.

Gary was sitting on the front porch, smoking a cigarette and looking like he had just woken up, even though it was the middle of the afternoon. He was wearing a faded red T-shirt and khaki pants with a hole in the knee. "I'm looking for a babysitting job," I said, as a way of introducing myself. "I'm good with kids and I'm around here all summer—days, weekends, whatever."

He looked up at me, cupped a hand over his brow and squinted into the sun.

"You're kidding. I told the agency I was looking for a nanny and they send me some underage jailbait. Haven't they heard about child labor laws up here?"

"I'm not with an agency," I said, objecting to being called "underage" more than "jailbait." "I live up the road and I'm looking for work."

"Strange," he said. "I was just sitting here wondering when are they going to send someone over to help and then here you are, walking down the lane like an answer to prayer. Jesus. That's some coincidence."

"I'm just looking for a job," I said.

"Well, it's your lucky day," he said, "because I'm hiring. My wife got a call to be in L.A.; I'm on deadline and I need some full-time help around here while I work."

All I could see were dollar signs filling up a long, dull summer. "I'm available all day," I said. "No problem."

"I mean it," he said. "I don't work normal hours. I may be home but if that door is closed"—he pointed to the shed behind the house—"I'm working. It is strictly do-not-disturb time around here. Got it?"

I assured him that long hours were no problem, trying to sound confident.

"Sorry. You just caught me off guard. I was expecting an agency nanny. You know, like Mary Poppins, someone older. I'm going to really need you to run the show around here. I hope you can handle it."

For the first several weeks Gary worked long hours in the tiny shed behind the house, coming into the main house for drinks and food, and I guess to sleep. As late as I stayed, I never saw him go into the back bedroom. In fact, in those early weeks, I rarely saw him at all. The girls started camp at Sunny Day, and after dropping them off I would spend my mornings cleaning up from the night before, collecting ashtrays or anything that was used as an ashtray—plate, bottle, coffee mug—and trying to re-establish some sense of order in the house. By mid-afternoon, once everything was straightened up, I would make a sandwich for Gary and leave it in the fridge, and then head out to the porch, picking up anything from the shelves to read that looked interesting.

"What the hell are you reading that crap for?" Gary asked, shaking his head at me. I was engrossed in a fat old dog-eared copy of *Valley of the Dolls* and didn't even hear him come out on the porch. "That stuff will rot your brain." He went back in the house and came out with another book and tossed it at me. *Madame Bovary*. "Try that one," he said.

A few days later there was a book left on the kitchen table with a note: TRY THIS ONE. As if it were a favorite recipe. *Anna Karenina*.

"Thanks for the books," I said. I was sitting on the couch watching Gary as he pored over the shelves looking for something. He had been working for almost two weeks straight, long days with barely any breaks.

"Sure," he said. "Girls your age just want to read about love, lust, and social climbing, right? God, even brooding Heathcliff is better than what you were reading."

He had a deep voice and everything he said came out in short, staccato beats that sounded like he was giving orders.

Girls my age? I wasn't sure what he meant by that. I was a new sixteen, having just turned in my braces, given up my glasses for contacts, and replaced my training bra with one bought in the ladies' department, a 36C Playtex in a shade called "Nude."

"I thought Heathcliff was creepy," I said. "Too obsessed."

He looked at me, surprised. "Really?"

"But the women seemed real to me," I said. "I mean for happening such a long time ago."

I had been watching Gary since I started working for him. I always seemed drawn to where he was in a room, to his face, the movement of his lips under his mustache, and yet now that he was standing so close to me, I found it difficult to even look at him to make eye contact.

"So, what's the famous writer working on?" I asked. "Is it top secret or can you tell me?"

He laughed and sat down next to me. It was one of the first times he seemed relaxed. "Famous? Where did you get that idea?"

"Well, these posters of your plays." I pointed at the wall.

"Believe me," he said. "I am not famous. Not even close. I had promise once, when I was young."

"You're not old," I said. "And your wife is really famous, too. I recognize her, I've seen her on a ton of commercials. You're both so successful."

He laughed and told me about how he and Sherry met at college. How he was going to write plays, and she was going to act in them. They had some early success with a small rep company; he won a few student prizes. And then, after the girls were born, Sherry started landing TV commercials and now wanted to pursue television jobs in L.A.

"Sherry wanted me to go out with her this summer, to spend time pitching scripts to television producers, if you can believe that. As if that's how I wanted to spend my summer vacation, time when I'm not teaching, when I could be writing, to go sit in meetings in L.A." He shook his head and got up from the couch.

I didn't say anything. If the Singers weren't successful, then I didn't know much about success.

Sherry usually called from the coast around bedtime to talk to the girls. I would ask if she wanted me to put Gary on, to go knock on his door in the little house in the backyard. "Oh, don't bother him," she said. "He can always call me back later. You know what a bear he is if you disturb him while he's working." She acted as if we both knew him well enough to get the joke.

Most nights I stayed at the house till around nine, leaving after dark, when the girls had fallen asleep and I had put the house back in order. Gary and I began to fall into an easy habit of talking in the evenings, after the girls were in bed, when he came back in for a beer-and-cigarette break. Usually we talked about books or what he was working on. One night he told me his characters felt flat, that he wanted to give them more of an edge. I was working my way through his recommended reading, on to D. H. Lawrence, and told him the one thing I'd noticed was that everyone wanted something they couldn't have, and that's what kept the story interesting.

"What do you want that you don't have?" he asked. I always felt uncomfortable when he asked me such a direct question.

"That's too easy," I said. "It's like that genie question with the three wishes. The real answer isn't about the wishes but about finding a way to make those things come true yourself, so you don't need the genie."

"You're a very strange girl," he said. "Very strange."

The night Gary finished his rough draft there was a celebration. He bought a sheet cake from Forest Bakery, and for the first time that summer he stayed at the dinner table after he ate instead of bolting back to his office. "I'm a long way from finished," he said. "But the first hurdle's cleared."

At the table he told stories, making the girls laugh as he acted out all the parts. We put birthday candles in the cake; he made a toast—"to a productive summer!"—his beer bottle thudding against our plastic cups. I watched him across the table, and I could feel that he was watching me too.

After the girls were asleep he stretched out on the couch and seemed in no hurry to return to work. "I borrowed your line about the genie," he said. "About how we make our own dreams and wishes."

I asked him if I were a character in his play, thrilled at the idea of being written about. "Not exactly," he said. "But the line worked great." He told me how the two characters finally wind up together in a seedy motel reading passages out loud from *Song of Songs*.

"The Bible?" I asked. "They meet for the last time and they sit around reading the Bible?"

Gary laughed. "Sure," he said. "Best erotic poetry around." He reached past me toward the bottom shelf. I watched as he flipped through see-through pages and then read to me about alabaster skin, lovers anointing each other with oil, about sleeping with an awakened heart, and listening for a lover's knock. "It doesn't get much better than this," he said as he closed the book. "If you're ever having a tryst in a motel room, always go for the Gideon. This stuff is a bigger turn-on than any in-room movie or one of those magic finger beds."

"I'll remember that," I said, not really knowing what to say—trysts, lovers, motel rooms. But I filed it in that place in my brain where everything he ever told me went.

"I need another beer," he said. "It feels great to finally kick back a little."

"I'll have one too," I said.

He raised an eyebrow, like he was looking at me differently, or for the first time.

"It's a celebration, right?" I asked.

Gary followed close behind as I walked into the kitchen. I felt his breath on my shoulder. Instead of opening the fridge, I turned to face him and put my arms around his neck.

"You girls start young up here," he said. He laughed and if I had thought about it, I would have said he was nervous. I didn't tell him that I hadn't started much of anything yet. Instead I kissed him. Hard. His hand slid up my thigh, to my hips, and then he pulled me closer. I was pinned against the refrigerator, his full weight leaning against me. At that moment I wanted to please him, and more than that, I wanted to impress him with an expertise I didn't possess. I took one of his fingers slowly into my mouth and I heard him whisper something that sounded like *Oh god.*

He reached under my sundress and rolled my underpants down until they dropped to the floor. I kicked them away with my foot and Gary knelt to retrieve them. They were white cotton with small pink flowers, and he swung them over his head like a lasso. I laughed, a white flag of surrender, and I knew then that time would be measured by before and after, there would be no going back.

The summer passed quickly. Quiet kisses on the front porch, the feel of his moustache on my shoulder. The pancake house in Ellenville, where a waitress mistook me for his daughter. The nights we sat around, a blanket wrapped around us, talking. He asked me questions I could never answer: Did I know that I was sexy? What do we think we're doing here? How did this happen? I remember laughing, like I was used to these kinds of quandaries. And Gary told me stories; it was like Arabian Nights. He filled my head with love stories every night, not many with happy endings. I cried over Tristan and Isolde, when Gary said that love was the true pain of living.

Sherry called one Sunday morning at eleven. I answered the phone sleepily. The girls were out playing who knows where; Gary was probably at work. I had fallen asleep on the couch, tired from staying up all night with him the night before. Good for you, she said, for keeping an eye on things while she was away. Thank God I was there; there was no way he could keep it together on his own. We both laughed then, in the shared grown-up way women laugh when they're talking about men.

We sat outside on the lawn. It was late in the evening, a dark summer night, the cicadas buzzing their constant drone in the background. We were in a lawn chair, a chaise lounge with fat woven straps of orange and green. I wore only Gary's Fordham T-shirt, blue and faded. I sat between his legs, a Mexican blanket thrown over us. His hands felt warm and they slid easily against my skin. We were looking up at the sky, the ropes of stars, the chaos of dark and light, and he pointed with his finger, traced a line to the North Star.

"Do you see that?" he asked, pointing toward a cluster of white blots to the left. "It's Cassiopeia."

He traced a *W* above my head in the air, mirrored it across my back with his lips.

"Do you know about her?" he asked. "Cassiopeia?" He moved the blanket closer around us. I shook my head, moving it left to right against his chest.

"It's from mythology," he said. "She was a vain queen who angered the gods; she felt her young daughter was too good for an arranged marriage."

I felt the pressure of his hand against my stomach. Once, in grade school, I visited a planetarium, a dark place with a curved sloping roof that made me feel dizzy and off balance every time I looked up at the stars. I felt the same way as Gary's hand travelled over me. I closed my eyes.

"When she died, the gods chained her to a throne and placed her in the sky. You should really see it in the fall; it's much better then. You could get lost in it."

I was lost in it here, lost to the universe above my head, between my legs—I made no distinction.

"Half the year she hangs upside down, not a *W* anymore. Instead it's more like the letter *M*. It was supposed to be a warning, a punishment for her vanity, to let people know what happened when you disobeyed the gods. The Romans called her 'The Woman of the Chair'."

I felt the warmth of his palm against my hip bone. I had become the woman of the chair, feeling every inch like a woman, my eyes closed, not looking up at the star-patterned warning.

We should have heard the tires on the gravel, the sound of the car door, the precise click of heels against the slate path. Instead, I was lost, dizzy with the entire universe expanding inside me.

"What the hell is this?"

She was beautiful, professionally beautiful: tall, tan, sleek as a racehorse. She wore a linen sundress, crisp and unwrinkled, even after the long drive from the airport. She stood in front of us at the foot of the chair. I watched as she looked around: wine glasses, small circle of candles, and me, pulling my knees to my chest, trying to stretch the T-shirt, to cover myself, to shrink inside it.

Sherry looked me up and down once and then turned her full attention to Gary.

"A local girl?" she asked. "I'm working my ass off on the coast and you're here, fucking a local girl?"

He stood up quickly, pulling the Mexican blanket around his waist. "It's not what it looks like. I can explain," he said. "This is not what it seems."

"Not what it seems?" she said, repeating him, her voice getting louder with each word. Her articulation was perfect, her intonation pitched close to outrage. "What it seems, Gary, is pathetic." She shook her head, and her hair moved softly from side to side. "I can't believe it. I should have known. I'm hard at work and you're up here with the babysitter." She sneered at him, revealing a straight row of gleaming white teeth that shone brightly in the candlelight.

"It's nothing," he said. "Believe me. I know it looks bad, but it's really nothing."

"The babysitter," she said again. "I should have known. What a fucking cliché."

They were oblivious of me in their argument and I stepped back, away from the warm circle of candlelight, toward the road that led home. I walked the next two miles along an unlit country road with no shoulder, my feet bare, wearing only Gary's T-shirt and a new heavy feeling of shame.

The Singers packed up soon after that and for an entire year the bungalow stood empty, no sign of their return. And then at the start of the summer season, the time of year when local grocery stores began to stock postcards, picnic foods, and county maps, I went back. I walked down the road to the small blue bungalow and hung around the periphery of the yard, hoping to catch sight of him. I couldn't help myself. I saw trash bags set out for the Dumpster, a can of Budweiser on the stoop, tire marks in the dirt driveway: signs of life. Then the creak of the screen door, and a clean-shaven man stepped out and waved.

"I'm looking for the family who stays here during the summer," I said, approaching the porch. "I'm the babysitter."

"They're in Spain," he said from the doorway. "Madrid. Gary got a grant for the summer, took the whole family."

I nodded, getting the picture pretty quickly that this guy would not be needing a babysitter. He told me his name was Matt, a friend of Gary's from the city, a graphic artist renting the house and studio while the Singers were in Spain.

"So, do you come with the house?" he asked with an easy smile. "I could use a tour guide around here, someone who knows the back roads, who can clean up and whatnot."

I shook my head.

"That's too bad," he said. "I can see now why Gary spent so much time up here."

Later that summer I met a boy my own age. At night we lined our bodies up close in the dark, skin touching, and fit together perfectly, like interlocking puzzle pieces: at mouth, hip, and heart.

Two weeks after my high school graduation, at the start of the following summer, Gary called.

"I'm up for the weekend," he said. "Can I see you?"

It had been almost two years since that night in the backyard. "Please," he said. "I really want to see you again. I have something for you."

Not much had changed. The house had a musty smell from being closed up most of the year. Gary was standing by the kitchen window. I knew he was watching as I walked up.

"Look at you, all grown up," he said, laughing, when I walked into the kitchen. "You probably have your driver's license by now."

"Too traumatized by driver's ed," I said. But he was right; I had changed. I wore my hair shorter, plucked my eyebrows thin, smoked—though not very well—and dressed in a way I imagined looked older and sexy: white halter top, raspberry lip gloss, denim short shorts and high-heeled sandals that were impossible to walk in.

He hugged me warmly. "How about a beer?" he asked. We sat at the table, across from each other like polite strangers. "You look great," he said again. "All grown up."

I smiled at him; I couldn't help it. My mouth hurt from smiling; it had a mind of its own. I pretended to cough just to have an excuse to cover my mouth with my hand.

"Wait here," he said. "Don't move, I have something for you." He returned with a set of books, a box with a thesaurus and dictionary.

"In honor of your graduation," he said. "They'll come in handy when you go away to school." He sat down across from me at the table and pushed the box toward me.

I looked at the spines, red, straight, and collegiate, and resisted the urge to run my fingers down them. "Thanks," I said. "But I'm not going to college."

He looked a little stunned. "What do you mean?"

"I'm getting married," I told him. "In two weeks."

"Married? You're not even eighteen—are you pregnant?"

"I am *too* eighteen." That was the most mature response I could think of, and at that moment it felt like a very important fact. "My birthday was last month."

"Is it money? There are grants, all sorts of things." Gary got up from the table, running his fingers through his thinning hair. "Please don't tell me you didn't even bother to apply."

"It's love," I said. "I met someone. I fell in love."

"Love." He said it as if he were describing a critical condition. "How old is he—eighteen, too?"

I nodded.

"That's not love," he said. "That's hormones. Just because he can get it up three times a night doesn't mean he loves you, believe me."

"You don't know anything about this," I said.

"Maybe. But what I do know is that you're probably making the biggest mistake of your life. Don't do it. Come with me."

"What?"

He reached across the table for me. I had never seen him look so serious. "I'm leaving Sherry," he said. "I came here to tell you that. I got an offer from Chicago, an artist in residency for a year. It doesn't pay much but there's housing and time for me to write."

"Chicago?"

"It would be great for you," he said. "You would meet actors, maybe take some classes. Chicago is a great city, I know you'd love it. And we could be together."

"I'm getting married," I said again, drawing my hands away. "In two weeks. Your timing sucks."

"You're too smart to get married," he said. "Don't throw it all away and ruin your life."

That was the first time someone had called me smart. I tried to picture us then: Gary writing famous plays, maybe I would take up painting or sculpting, the two of us living together in a cool apartment in the city, throwing fancy dinners and cocktail parties.

"Besides," he added, "you're going to make a lousy wife." He went to the kitchen sink and lit a cigarette. "You were always so absent-minded. The house was never picked up. I would come in, the kids would be playing in the yard, you didn't know how to cook, and I would find you over there," he said, pointing toward the couch. "Curled up like a kitten, your nose in a book, oblivious to the squalor around you.

"I know you," he added. "You're too much like me; you live in your own head. You're never going to cut it as a wife."

"Thanks a lot," I said. He caught me looking down the hall, toward the back bedroom, his bedroom. I remembered the nights I crept in softly, my bare feet against the hardwoods, trying not to let the floors squeak and wake the kids.

"Oh no," he said. "I know what you're thinking. Being good in bed does not qualify you as a wife." He laughed. "In fact, if anything, just the opposite is true."

I thought about my wedding shower, the one my girlfriends gave me, the boxes of pots and pans, the toaster oven, the blender, and the only things that interested me were the lingerie—two sets of see-through babydoll nightgowns, black and red, with matching panties. I worried Gary might be right.

"It's not going to work," he said, sensing my doubts. "You'll never go to school. You'll get pregnant. And you'll end up right back here in this town. It's the oldest story in the book."

It sounded like he already had me wearing tube tops, living at the trailer park, and drawing a monthly government check. Like I would never escape the poor country town I came from.

"Oh really?" I said, gathering up my purse, getting ready to leave. "More cliché than fucking the babysitter?"

It was two weeks until my wedding. The florist had the standing order for fresh-cut daisies; I had my final fitting for the dress; the invitations with their two white slender-necked swans had been sent out to eighty of our closest friends and family members. Gary put his hands on my shoulders, and I felt their weight pressing on me.

We stared at each other for a long time without speaking. When he finally moved toward me, I turned away and he put his lips close to my ear. "I am sorry," he said. "We really did have something. I haven't stopped thinking about you;

I never stopped." He stepped in closer, put his arms around my waist.

"And after Chicago?" I whispered.

"After? I don't know, there will be things to take care of…" His words trailed off, his head buried in my hair, his fingers at the base of my neck loosening the knot of my halter top.

"But I'm getting married," I said again. This time with less conviction.

"This will be better than marriage," he said. "Trust me."

I turned and looked at him. He made a face, as if he knew he could have said something better, more original. He even laughed a little. And I laughed with him. We both laughed and I felt like I had lost my mind. A temporary insanity and then a sense of panic. I pushed him back and stepped away. "No, I really can't."

"Fine," he said. He took the dictionary set from the table and tossed it in the corner. "You won't be needing those, I guess." The books landed with a hollow-sounding thud.

I shook my head. "It didn't have to go like this," I said. "Sometimes people fall in love, sometimes things don't work out. End of story."

"Wait." He reached into his back pocket and took out his wallet. "Before you go, I have something for you. Consider it an early wedding present."

"I don't need your money."

He pulled out two twenties and tried to put them in my hands. "Don't think of it as money. Think of it as bus fare. To Chicago."

"I don't want it," I said.

"Please," he said. "Keep it. You might need it one day. Consider it an escape hatch, an emergency fund for when things don't work out. Come whenever you're ready. I'll be waiting."

"They *will* work out," I said, hoping it was true. "I'm in love."

"Sure," he said. "Absolutely. Chance always favors young love."

Gary went to Chicago and eventually wrote a play about our relationship, one that was mostly true, except our ages were changed—I was older, he was younger. The critics hated it. They called it narcissistic and exploitative, an unbelievable Pygmalion retelling dismissed as male fantasy. To my knowledge, it was never produced again. In his version, he was much harder on himself than on me. I was treated kindly, with a light and gentle touch and something that read like love. In his play, he gave me the last line, a virtuous head-held-high kind of ending, with a maturity and wisdom well beyond my scope.

In my story, there is a different ending. A truth that is harder to admit: I slept with him one more time and walked away, forty dollars tucked into my back pocket, carrying my high-heeled shoes, finding a new freedom that time in bare feet as I made my way home.

Acknowledgments

I must recognize and thank my George Mason University Graduate Creative Writing instructors: Richard Bausch, Alan Cheuse, Stephen Goodwin, and Susan Shreve—mentors, all. Big thanks to early literary editors for taking a chance, including Natalie Danford, John Kulka, Carol Shields, Cressida Leyshon, and Nicole Arthur and Joyce Jones of *The Washington Post*, and to Jennie Dunham and Rolph Blythe for believing. To the dedicated staff at Stillhouse Press, including Director of Operations William Miller; tireless graduate students Meghan L. McNamara and Marcos L. Martínez; eagle-eyed copy editor Jules Hucke; and the visionary Dallas Hudgens, Scott W. Berg, and Stephen Goodwin: thank you. Nothing but gratitude goes to publicity pro Lauren Cerand; to Caroline Leavitt for her immediate social networking support; and to Mary Kay Zuravleff for her thorough and heartfelt reading of my work.

Finally, these stories would not have been possible without my almost two-decade adventure with the extremely talented members of the Rotisserie Writers Group: Scott W. Berg, Robyn Goodwin, Corrine Gormont, and Dallas Hudgens—my lifeline, my creative outlet, my open door to all writing possibilities: thank you.

QUESTIONS FOR DISCUSSION

1. In the story "Helen on 86ᵗʰ Street," what do you think of Vita burning all the letters she has written to her father? Is she losing more than she is gaining in this ritual?

2. In "Helen on 86ᵗʰ Street," what do you think the theater and performing represent to Vita? Do you think they will be important to her character after the story is over?

3. Mr. Dodd is not the most encouraging of drama teachers, even after Vita gets the role of Helen. Have people in your life discouraged your art or your dreams?

4. Vita can easily verbalize what she wants in life: "to be Helen, to have my father come back." Do you think that as people age they lose the ability to express their deepest dreams and desires? Why?

5. In the story "Tryst and Doubt," Stephanie attempts to educate her insecure sister about the futility of expecting true love. Does Marie get it, or is she truly a "hopeless romantic"? Which sister would you rather be?

6. Some writers give us exemplary characters who show us how to be or how to act in the world. Others, not so much. When reading fiction, do you prefer to read about characters who get it right or those who get it wrong? Why?

7. Many of the stories in this collection seem to take a dim view of romantic love. In "Local Girl," Gary sarcastically says, "Chance always favors young love." Do you think these stories hold out any hope for happy endings?

8. In these fourteen stories we see many different women and girls coming of age at many different stages of life. Is there one character you relate to or sympathize with most? Why?

9. In the story "Visitation Rights," do you believe Missy really has the gift? What do you think happens in the final scene? Have you ever experienced a paranormal event?

10. Adultery is a theme in many of these stories. Do you think there is a double standard for men and women regarding infidelity?

11. What role does the past—nostalgia, regret, memories—play in the lives of the characters in these stories? How does it drive their actions in the present? Do you often think about events and emotions from your own past?

12. These stories are full of complicated mother/daughter relationships. Do you think these daughters want to be like their mothers, or do you think they are trying to escape from their mothers' shadows? Does this theme resonate with you?

13. The stories "Helen on 86th Street" and "Still Life" are set in New York City, while "Visitation Rights" and "Local Girl" are placed in more rural settings. Does the location of the story make a difference? Would the main characters be different people if their stories took place in different settings?

14. Many of the characters in *Helen on 86th Street and Other Stories* find themselves in situations far outside of their comfort zone. What have you done that took you out of your comfort zone? What obstacles did you face and what did you gain from the experience?